Dear Reader,

People often ask how I got my start as a writer. My first books were romance novels for Bantam's Loveswept line. Although the romance genre might seem quite different from the suspense I write now, I've found that the two genres actually have many similarities.

For me, every good story has two important ingredients: characters to root for and a mystery to unravel—whether it's an unsolved crime or that bewildering emotion that perplexes us most of all—love. Even the most intricate murder plot can't compare to the complex inner workings of the human heart.

One of my very first books was *McKnight in Shining Armor.* Heroine Kelsie Connors is struggling to keep it all together. She has two "high-energy" kids, a house filled with animals, and several jobs as she tries to provide for everyone. One day, there's an embarrassing (I don't want to give it away!) mix-up at her meeting with advertising executive Alec

McKnight. He can barely keep the smirk off his exceedingly handsome face, flustering Kelsie. Just when she's sure she's lost both the account and a chance for a date with Alex, he shows up on her doorstep, hoping to help this woman who's obviously in need of assistance. Kelsie's already smitten with his deep blue eyes and chivalrous demeanor, but can she possibly add one more complication to her already chaotic life?

I loved writing about Kelsie and Alec all those years ago, and I hope that you'll find them as enjoyable now as I did at the start of my writing career.

All my best,

Tami Hoag

Tami Hoag

Praise for the Bestsellers of Tami Hoag

THE ALIBI MAN

"Captivating thriller...[Elena] is a heroine readers will want to see more of." —*Publishers Weekly*

"Hard to put down." —*The Washington Post*

"A superbly taut thriller. Written in a staccato style that will have readers racing through the pages...Will leave readers breathless and satisfied." —*Booklist*

"A suspenseful tale, with a surprising ending; the author once again has constructed a hard-hitting story with interesting characters and a thrilling plot."
—*Midwest Book Review*

"Elena Estes [is] one of Hoag's most complicated, difficult and intriguing characters....Hoag enhances a tight mystery plot with an over-the-shoulder view of the Palm Beach polo scene, giving her readers an up-close-and-personal look at the rich and famous.... *The Alibi Man* is her best work to date."
—*BookReporter.com*

"An engrossing story and a cast of well-drawn characters." —Minneapolis *Star Tribune*

"[Hoag] gets better with every book. One of the tautest thrillers I have read for a long while."
—*Bookseller* (U.K.)

"Hoag certainly knows how to build a plot and her skill has deservedly landed her on bestseller lists numerous times." —*South Florida Sun-Sentinel*

"Hoag has a winner in this novel where she brings back Elena Estes.... Hoag is the consummate storyteller and creator of suspense." —*Mystery News*

"Tami Hoag weaves an intricate tale of murder and deception.... A very well-written and thought-out murder/mystery. Hoag is able to keep you guessing and you'll be left breathless until all the threads are unwoven and the killer is revealed." —FreshFiction.com

PRIOR BAD ACTS

"A snappy, scary thriller." —*Entertainment Weekly*

"Stunning... Here [Hoag] stands above the competition, creating complex characters who evolve more than those in most thrillers. The breathtaking plot twists are perfectly paced in this compulsive page-turner." —*Publishers Weekly* (starred review)

"A chilling thriller with a romantic chaser."
—New York *Daily News*

"A first-rate thriller with an ending that will knock your socks off." —*Booklist*

"An engrossing thriller with plenty of plot twists and a surprise ending." —*OK!* magazine

"A chilling tale of murder and mayhem." —*BookPage*

"The in-depth characterization and the unrelenting suspense are what makes *Prior Bad Acts* an outstanding read. Gritty and brutal at times, *Prior Bad Acts* delivers a stunning novel of murder, vengeance and retribution. . . . Riveting and chilling suspense."
—*Romance Reviews Today*

KILL THE MESSENGER

"Excellent pacing and an energetic plot heighten the suspense. . . . Enjoyable." —*Chicago Tribune*

"Everything rings true, from the zippy cop-shop banter, to the rebellious bike messenger subculture, to the ultimate, heady collision of Hollywood money, politics, and power." —Minneapolis *Star Tribune*

"Hoag's usual crisp, uncluttered storytelling and her ability to make us care about her characters triumph in *Kill the Messenger*." —Fort Lauderdale *Sun-Sentinel*

"A perfect book. It is well written, and it has everything a reader could hope for.... It cannot be put down.... Please don't miss this one." —*Kingston Observer*

"[A] brisk read...it demonstrates once again why [Hoag's] so good at what she does."
—*San Francisco Chronicle*

"Action-filled ride...a colorful, fast-paced novel that will keep you guessing." —*Commercial Appeal*

"High-octane suspense...Nonstop action moves the story forward at a breath-stealing pace, and the tension remains high from beginning to end.... Suspense at its very best." —*Romance Reviews Today*

"Hoag's loyal readers and fans of police procedural suspense novels will definitely love it." —*Booklist*

"*Kill the Messenger* will add to [Hoag's] list of winners.... This is a fast-moving thriller with a great plot and wonderful characters. The identity of the killer is a real surprise." —*Daily American*

"Engaging...the triumph of substance over style... character-driven, solidly constructed thriller."

—*Publishers Weekly*

"Hoag upholds her reputation as one of the hottest writers in the suspense genre with this book, which not only has a highly complex mystery, multilayered suspense and serpentine plot, but also great characterizations...an entertaining and expertly crafted novel not to be missed." —CurledUp.com

DARK HORSE

"A thriller as tightly wound as its heroine...Hoag has created a winning central figure in Elena....Bottom line: Great ride." —*People*

"This is her best to date....[A] tautly told thriller."

—Minneapolis *Star Tribune*

"Hoag proves once again why she is considered a queen of the crime thriller."

—Charleston *Post and Courier*

"A tangled web of deceit and double-dealing makes for a fascinating look into the wealthy world of horses juxtaposed with the realistic introspection of one very troubled ex-cop. A definite winner." —*Booklist*

"Anyone who reads suspense novels regularly is acquainted with Hoag's work—or certainly should be. She's one of the most consistently superior suspense and romantic suspense writers on today's bestseller lists. A word of warning to readers: don't think you know whodunit 'til the very end." —Clute *Facts*

"Suspense, shocking violence, and a rip-roaring conclusion—this novel has all the pulse-racing touches that put Tami Hoag books on bestseller lists and crime fans' reading lists." —Baton Rouge *Advocate Magazine*

"Full of intrigue, glitter, and skullduggery . . . [Hoag] is a master of suspense." —*Publishers Weekly*

"Her best to date, an enjoyable read, and a portent of even better things to come." —*Grand Rapids Press*

"A complex cerebral puzzle that will keep readers on the edge until all the answers are revealed."
—*Midwest Book Review*

"To say that Tami Hoag is the absolute best at what she does is a bit easy since she is really the only person who does what she does. . . . It is a testament to Hoag's skill that she is able to go beyond being skillful and find the battered hearts in her characters, and capture their beating on the page. . . . A superb read."
—*Detroit Free Press*

BANTAM TITLES BY TAMI HOAG

The Alibi Man

Prior Bad Acts

Kill the Messenger

Dark Horse

Dust to Dust

Ashes to Ashes

A Thin Dark Line

Guilty as Sin

Night Sins

Dark Paradise

Cry Wolf

Still Waters

Lucky's Lady

The Last White Knight

Straight from the Heart

Tempestuous/The Restless Heart

Taken by Storm

Heart of Dixie

Mismatch

Man of Her Dreams

TAMI HOAG

McKnight in Shining Armor

BANTAM BOOKS

Sale of this book without a front cover may be unauthorized.
If this book is coverless, it may have been reported to the publisher
as "unsold or destroyed" and neither the author nor the publisher
may have received payment for it.

McKnight in Shining Armor is is a work of fiction.
Names, characters, places, and incidents either are the product
of the author's imagination or are used fictitiously.
Any resemblance to actual persons, living or dead, events,
or locales is entirely coincidental.

2009 Bantam Books Mass Market Edition

Copyright © 1988 by Tami Hoag

All rights reserved.

Published in the United States by Bantam Books,
an imprint of The Random House Publishing Group,
a division of Random House, Inc., New York.

BANTAM BOOKS and the rooster colophon
are registered trademarks of Random House, Inc.

Originally published in the United States in paperback by
Bantam Books, in 1988.

978-0-553-59311-2

Cover art: Alan Ayers
Cover photo of skaters: copyright © LWA/Getty Images

Printed in the United States of America

www.bantamdell.com

2 4 6 8 9 7 5 3 1

McKnight in Shining Armor

ONE

"DAMN!"

"Jeffrey Connors, I do *not* want to hear that kind of language in this house," Kelsie Connors said, admonishing her nine-year-old son while trying to dry the fingernail polish on her right hand as she attempted to butter a slice of toast with the left.

"But, Mom!" Jeffrey whined, peering at his mother over the myraid cereal boxes on the kitchen table. "My pencil broke and I have four math problems to finish and the bus is gonna be here in five minutes!"

Kelsie's toast fell from her plate to the floor, landing facedown. An orange tiger-striped cat darted out from beneath the table and ran off with it. Kelsie dropped her knife and heaved a sigh. Murphy's Law would have to strike full force today of all days, she thought.

An enormous dog with shaggy black and brown hair pushed open the basement door and bounded into the kitchen, his nails clicking on the linoleum floor. He gave two enthusiastic barks, reared up, and plopped his massive paws on the table, toppling the milk carton, which spewed its contents over five cereal boxes and two hand-quilted place mats that belonged in the dining room.

"Damn!" Kelsie bolted out of her chair, grabbed a dishtowel, and began sopping up the mess.

"Damn!" echoed the parrot from its cage in the dining room.

"Mom, you swore!" Jeffrey said, smiling.

"Who let Bronco in the house?" Kelsie asked in

a tone of voice that did not invite confession. The towel she had grabbed had stuck to her nail polish, and now the fingernails of her right hand were coated with fuzz.

Jeffrey pointed to his thirteen-year-old sister as she danced into the room, absorbed in singing her latest favorite song along with the radio.

"Elizabeth did!"

"I did not!" the pretty blond girl denied automatically, glaring at her little brother.

"Cease fire!" Kelsie yelled, dragging Bronco by the collar to the back door. She tried to avoid brushing against his body because he shed year round, and she was already dressed for her meeting at Glendenning Advertising in downtown Minneapolis—which promised to be the most important meeting she'd attend since starting her talent agency for animals two years before.

With the dog safely out in the fenced backyard, she turned back to her children. "Now, listen up. I'll be a little late tonight because they're shooting that tissue commercial at three o'clock. The number at the studio is on the bulletin board; don't call unless there's blood. There are cookies in the cookie jar; don't eat them all. Supper is at six. Don't forget, I have a party tonight."

Elizabeth frowned. "I thought you were quitting that job, Mom."

Kelsie crossed her fingers and held up both hands. "As soon as I land the Van Bryant deal, sweetheart. If the people at Glendenning Advertising decide to use Darwin the chimp in the Van Bryant Department Store campaign, the first thing I'll do is turn in my Naughty Nighties home party kit."

When her marriage to Jack Connors disintegrated, Kelsie had found herself in a deep hole. She'd been twenty-nine years old with no solid work experience, two children to raise, and a mini-menagerie to feed. She'd kept a roof over their heads and food in the cupboards by giving lingerie sales parties. Then one day it hit her. Why not let her pets earn their own keep? The idea had mushroomed into a business—Monkey Business—named for Kelsie's first outside client, Darwin the chimp.

She had enjoyed a certain amount of success with the business, but she still was struggling a bit financially. This was her make-it-or-break-it year. With the Van Bryant account under her belt, she would definitely make it. Without the Van Bryant deal, she could end up working as a clerk at the 7-Eleven again.

Darwin the chimpanzee, dressed in a red polo shirt and jogging shorts, sat staring morosely at Steve Randall, an account executive for Glendenning. Steve and Kelsie, who had met while working on a series of ads for a local children's wear store, and Darwin and his owner, Millard Krispin, sat in the reception area outside the office of Glendenning vice-president Alexander L. McKnight.

"How's Darwin feeling, Millard?" Kelsie asked the wiry little man sitting beside the chimp.

"Ooh," Millard cooed, a worried look pinching his sharp features. He combed back a lock of unkempt brown hair and pushed his glasses up on his nose with his ring finger. "I don't know, Kelsie. He hasn't been himself since he worked that circus theme party at the Sons of Norway lodge in Coon Rapids."

"Cute little guy," remarked Mr. McKnight's secretary, Ms. Bond. Ms. Bond, Kelsie noted, had a voice like Yosemite Sam and bore a rather startling resemblance to Hulk Hogan.

Kelsie smiled and nodded, smoothing her hands over her khaki skirt and glancing at her watch. They had been waiting nearly half an hour. If they had to sit much longer, Darwin was bound to lose his patience.

"Forget it, Vena!" a male voice suddenly boomed from the other side of McKnight's door.

Kelsie jumped. Ms. Bond abandoned her typing, leaned toward Kelsie conspiratorially, and said, "His ex."

"Alec," the woman pleaded. "How can you turn me down?"

"Like this: No!"

Kelsie gulped. He sounded like the kind of man who kicked puppies out of his path. Steve had hinted he might be a hard man to sell an animal act to. Now they had to sell it to him on the heels of a fight with his ex-wife. Terrific.

Ms. Bond lit a cigarette. "Don't let this tragic act of hers fool you. She's a barracuda in Gucci pumps. Walks all over him, then has the gall to come waltzing in here asking for money for her sleazy boyfriend's 'fashion import' business. Har! Who ever heard of fashion originals from Colombia? If that slimeball isn't a drug dealer, I'm Hulk Hogan!"

Feigning a coughing fit, Kelsie turned toward Steve.

"Alec, please!" the woman begged. "Won't you give me anything?"

"Vena," Alexander McKnight responded in a voice laced with cynical amusement. "If you were on fire, I wouldn't lend you my phone to call nine one one."

Steve turned pale and sat back in his chair.

"You bastard!" the woman yelled. "You made me fly all the way from New York just to turn me down!"

Alec McKnight laughed. "Sorry. Too bad you had to put all those miles on your broom for nothing."

The unmistakable sound of a face being

slapped echoed into the reception area, then the office door flew open and Vena McKnight stormed out. She was a beautiful woman with enormous black eyes and a wide, pouting mouth that gleamed with cherry-red lipstick. Her black hair was slicked back from her face. She paused only long enough to glare at Ms. Bond.

"Where's Randall?" Alexander McKnight roared over the intercom.

Ms. Bond stubbed out her cigarette and jabbed a button on the machine. "On his way in, Mr. McKnight."

Steve turned a shade of gray that matched the pinstripes of his navy blue suit. Kelsie reached up and straightened his tie. "Get a handle on it, Steve. We both need this job."

Alexander McKnight was sitting behind a large oak desk when they entered his office. He looked formidable, Kelsie thought, unapproachable, and intimidating. She couldn't decide whether his hair was black or brown, but it had red highlights, was fashionably cut, neatly combed, and parted on the left. His profile was almost hawkish as he scowled down at something on his desktop, eyes narrowed above high cheekbones, his mouth set in a tight line beneath a nose that was just barely aquiline enough to save it from being nondescript. Rising from his chair, he adjusted his dark double-breasted suit coat and regarded the peculiar foursome with eyes the exact shade of the deep sapphire blue of his silk tie.

On a scale of really bad moods, Alec thought, the one he was in now would have to rank about a mile and a half off the chart. Seeing Vena was enough to open wounds that hadn't fully healed. Having her pour salt on them might have been a masochist's idea of a great time, but it wasn't his. He felt raw and angry. The fuse of his temper was frayed so short, he couldn't have gotten a hold on it with a tweezers.

Rationally Alec knew he shouldn't go into a discussion about the new campaign for Glendenning's most important client in such a state of mind, but the mood he was in caused him to lose all capacity for rational reasoning. It didn't matter anyway, because he had already seen Steve Randall's ideas for the campaign and had decided against them. Cute ads with cuddly animals weren't Alec's style. He preferred sleek, polished, sophisticated advertising.

Meeting with a man and his monkey didn't appeal to him in the least right now. Of course, he thought, having to meet with *anyone* wouldn't appeal to him.

Then he laid eyes on the woman who completed the quartet.

Her thick shoulder-length honey-blond hair was clipped back at the sides with black combs. Big eyes the color of faded denim stared at him from beneath brows that were a couple of shades darker than her hair. Too sexy, he thought, groaning inwardly, amazed that he could be so totally distracted by her when he was in such a rotten mood. No question, she appealed to him— enough to make him temporarily forget the headache knifing through his temples, enough to make him temporarily forget there was a chimpanzee in his office. She appealed to him from the tip of her upturned nose right down to the tan suede boots beneath her safari-look skirt. Everything about her appealed to him, even her direct stare—which was not unlike the stares everyone else in the room was focusing on him, including the monkey.

Steve Randall stepped forward nervously to make a round of introductions. "Kelsie, this is Mr. McKnight. Mr. McKnight, Kelsie Connors, representing Mr. Krispin. Mr. Krispin, Mr. McKnight."

Alec reached out to shake Kelsie's hand—the hand with the furry fingernails, she realized. He gave them a brief, curious look, but took her long, fine-boned hand in his, looked directly into her eyes, and gave her a charming smile that revealed gleaming white teeth, two deep dimples in his cheeks, and the hint of a cleft in his chin.

Kelsie's heart flipped over like a beached salmon. She wouldn't have said Alexander McKnight was extraordinarily handsome; some women may not have found him at all handsome. But that smile...it transformed his face so completely that the contrast took Kelsie's breath away. It was mischievous and charming, boyish yet dangerously male. It was the kind of smile that must have saved him from dozens of spankings as a little boy, the kind of smile that opened doors for a man—boardroom and bedroom doors. It was cocky, playfully self-confident, and absolutely irresistible.

"*Miss* Connors?" he asked silkily, taking notice of the fact that she wasn't wearing a wedding ring.

"Yes." She just managed to resist the urge to laugh giddily.

"May I call you Kelsie? It's a lovely name," he said in a voice like velvet. No, she thought, it was more like satin—warm, smooth black satin, like satin sheets...

"Sure." She sighed as he let her hand go. It dropped like a stone, shaking her out of the trance his voice and thousand-watt smile had cast over her. She blushed furiously. The future of her business depended on this meeting. She couldn't very well let this man think she was some kind of bimbo, especially since she had always prided herself on her professionalism. "I mean, thank you, Mr. McKnight. Yes, please do call me Kelsie."

Encouraged by the looks his boss was giving

Kelsie, Steve grinned and said, "So, shall we get down to business, Alec?"

Alec shot him a scowl.

"M-Mr. McKnight," he corrected himself nervously, slinking down on a chair.

Alec gave Millard Krispin a pale smile and a brief handshake. The man appeared to have crawled out of a laundry basket. The chimp was better dressed. Better looking, too, Alec thought. Millard looked as if he were chronically nauseated. He wore a wrinkled white shirt with an ink-stained pocket full of ballpoint pens, ankle-length powder-blue polyester pants, and black half-boots. The sight was enough to bring Alec's headache back to his attention.

Millard leaned toward Kelsie as they all took seats. "No one introduced Darwin," he complained, hurt and offended.

Kelsie patted his clammy hand on the arm of the chair. "Mr. McKnight—"

His smile was instantaneous as he leaned his forearms on the desk. "Alec."

"Alec," Kelsie repeated, her cheeks heating. For Pete's sake, she hadn't blushed in years! She was reacting like a teenager with a hormone imbalance. Breaking eye contact with him, she gestured toward the chimp on Millard's lap. "This is Darwin, our star."

Alec nodded, his dark brows bobbing over his eyes. He wasn't quite sure how to respond.

"Say hello to the nice man, Darwin," Millard told the chimp. "Say, 'Hello, nice Mr. Mc-Knight,' " he went on in a childish voice. " 'Pleased to meet you.' "

The guy was slipping a few gears, Alec thought. Kelsie pinched the bridge of her nose between her thumb and forefinger, wondering if they had been wise in deciding to bring Darwin and Millard along. Steve had thought the chimp might be able to help their cause by charming McKnight. Darwin bared his teeth and hissed at Alec.

Alec sat back and cleared his throat. "I'm sure Steve has explained to you how we're handling this campaign, Kelsie, Mr. Krispin. Eugene Van Bryant, head of the Van Bryant chain of stores, has asked me to oversee the project personally. I've asked all our top people to come up with ideas for the campaign, ideas I will screen. Finally,

I will present what I consider to be the best of them to Mr. Van Bryant. The ultimate decision will be his."

"Have you had a chance to look at my ideas, Mr. McKnight?" Steve asked.

"Ah—yes, I have," Alec said, shuffling through the papers in front of him. "I'll be honest with you, Steve. They're not what I had in mind."

Kelsie's heart sank. If Alexander McKnight didn't like their idea, Kelsie figured she'd be selling lingerie at night until she was eighty.

"But I'm willing to listen," Alec added, catching himself staring at Kelsie Connors's mouth. It looked so soft. He wondered what it would taste like, then shook his head. How could he be thinking about kissing Kelsie Connors when he should be concentrating on business? How he could be thinking anything pleasant about women in general after his visit from Vena was beyond him.

"That's all I ask." Steve grinned, his spirits lifting. He scooted to the edge of his chair, brown eyes glowing. "I see an entire series of ads—print and video—with Darwin as the star. Just Darwin and Van Bryant merchandise, which, I might point out, is very cost effective. Compared to what we would have to pay models or actors, Darwin here works for peanuts, or, I should say, bananas."

"That's a valid point," Alec conceded, frowning in concentration as he doodled a nasty caricature of Vena on his ink blotter. "However, our main concern has to be the quality and tone of the ads. Van Bryant's has always appealed to a more sophisticated customer."

"True," Steve said. "But they're looking to broaden their customer base. Traditionally they've been thought of only as an upper-class chain. Now they want to capture those yuppie spending dollars, bring in the middle-class, white-collar baby boomers, and baby boomettes.

"The way I see it, they need an ad campaign with mass appeal, something that will make Van Bryant's seem friendly, welcoming, fun."

Darwin left his owner's lap for Kelsie's, wrapping one long hairy arm around her shoulders. He fingered the cameo she wore at the throat of her khaki cotton blouse. As comfortable with animals as she was with children, Kelsie smiled at him and gently tickled his tummy.

"What's more fun than a monkey?" Steve asked, smiling his most engaging smile.

Millard sat up, ready for a fight. "Darwin is not a monkey."

"Figure of speech," Steve said between clenched teeth.

Darwin became interested in the items on Alec's desk. He scooted forward on Kelsie's lap, his fingers reaching out to caress an appointment book, a rough pottery cup filled with pens, a heavy glass paperweight. Each piece he moved, Alec reached out and moved back.

"Animals are very hot right now," Steve continued. "Darwin could be to Van Bryant's what Spuds MacKenzie is to Budweiser. And I think the slogan is very catchy and adaptable to all of Van Bryant's merchandise." He held his hands up as if he were picturing the slogan on a billboard. " 'When it comes to fashion, don't monkey around. Van Bryant's.' "

Millard sucked in a horrified breath, drawing

everyone's attention. "Darwin is *not* a monkey!" he said emphatically.

Kelsie rushed to placate him, wishing—not for the first time—that Millard Krispin weren't so unbalanced. "Millard, like Steve said, it's just a figure of speech. I'm sure everyone will realize Darwin isn't a monkey. And you'll have to agree, 'Don't chimpanzee around' doesn't have quite the right ring to it."

Millard sat back, breathing heavily. "I guess you're right, Kelsie." He pushed his glasses up on his nose and leveled a serious look at Alec. "I'm sorry for my outburst, Mr. McKnight. I hope you understand I'm only looking out for Darwin's interests. I have to make sure he isn't exploited in any way."

"Of course." Alec nodded gravely, rubbing his temples. This guy belongs in a home for the chronically weird, he decided.

Kelsie reached for her briefcase as Darwin scrambled back to his owner's lap. "I have a file here with photos of Darwin's previous ad experience. While he hasn't worked on television, he's appeared in newspaper and regional magazine ads for children's clothes—which were done by your firm—Metro Animal Hospital, Tanner's Bookstores, and—" She popped open the lid on the case and her stomach did a cartwheel. Instead of files and papers and photographs, she found bras and garter belts. The words escaped her lips on a thready breath. "Naughty Nighties."

"I beg your pardon?" Alec leaned forward. He could have sworn she'd said "Naughty Nighties." How could a monkey advertise nighties? Now, Miss Connors herself...

Before she could slam the lid on the case, Darwin reached in and scooped out most of the contents. With a wild screech, he fired a frilly black bra at Alec slingshot style, catching him full across the face, then bounded across the room, flinging lingerie helter-skelter. Shrieking with delight, he pulled a pair of pink satin panties on over his head and leapt from the back of a cordovan leather sofa to hang from the drapery rod, slamming his feet against the window.

Millard was across the room in a flash, trying to coax the chimp down. "Darwin, what a bad boy you are! Come down and apologize to Mr. McKnight this instant!"

Steve fell back in his chair, groaning in defeat.

Alec peeled the bra off his face and stared at Kelsie. She had turned fuchsia. It was a good color on her, he thought. She cleared her throat, refusing to meet his gaze, and said, "I seem to have brought the wrong briefcase."

"Indeed." He was dying to know the story behind *this* briefcase, but he was sure he didn't want anyone else around when she told it. A pretty blonde with sexy eyebrows who carried a briefcase full of erotic undies. Intriguing lady.

Millard returned to his seat with Darwin in his arms, the panties still on the chimp's head. "I'm sorry, Mr. McKnight. Ordinarily Darwin is very professional. I don't know what came over him. He just lost his head, I think."

Alec surveyed his usually immaculate office with a pained smile. The drapery rod was bent so the drapes hung at drunken angles. There were monkey prints all over his view of the city. Garter belts hung from the potted palm like tinsel on a

Christmas tree. He felt the last fiber of his temper fuse split but held himself in rigid check.

"Well," he said, handing the bra back to Kelsie, "the sight of lacy underwear can do that to anyone."

"Darwin," Millard said to the chimp, who was holding up a see-through ivory lace teddy. "Apologize to Mr. McKnight. Say, 'I'm very sorry, Mr. McKnight!'" he said in his childish voice. "Say, 'I've been a very bad boy.' Go tell him. Go apologize and give him an 'I'm sorry' kiss."

Alec leaned back in his chair, on guard. "That's really not necessary, Mr. Krispin."

Millard ignored him, motioning Darwin to do as he was told. The chimpanzee grinned at him, draping the teddy over his owner's head, then scrambled onto Alec's desk, snatched up Alec's coffee mug, and, before Alec could bolt, tossed cold coffee in his face.

Steve wailed and squeezed his eyes shut, visions of the unemployment office dancing in his head.

"Oh, Darwin!" Millard scolded, grabbing the chimp. "No ice cream for you tonight!"

Alec snagged the teddy off Millard's head and

dried his face with it. Pain was pounding in his temples, and, pretty blonde or no pretty blonde, his temper was about to erupt like Mount St. Helens. First Vena the Vampire, now a madman and his maniac monkey. It was just too much.

"Mr. Krispin," he said threateningly, "will you please keep that animal under control?"

"Of course," Millard replied, trying to wrap his arms around Darwin as he sat back in his chair. The chimp wriggled around until he was sitting on Millard's shoulders and began playing his head like a bongo drum. "I think perhaps he's been eating too much refined sugar. What do you think?"

Alec stood, bracing his hands on his desk and leaning across it. He stared at Millard and said in a low, tight voice, "I think you've got a screw loose."

Millard gasped.

Kelsie snapped the lid shut on her briefcase of underwear and stood up, driven by a need to leave before she burst into tears and started reciting Chapter Eleven—the bankruptcy code. She had to get Millard and Darwin out of Alec Mc-

Knight's office before the chimp did any more damage. The last thing she needed was to get embroiled in a lawsuit. As it was, Millard was going to have to pay the cleaning bill on an expensive wool suit and replace a drapery rod.

"Perhaps it would be better if we discussed this at another time," she said, trying to cling to some tiny shred of hope, "without Darwin being present."

"But Kelsie—" Millard whined, cutting himself off at a murderous look from his agent.

Alec handed her the lace teddy. "I think not, Miss Connors. I believe I can safely say Van Bryant's would not be interested in a neurotic monkey with an underwear fetish."

"How dare you!" Millard exclaimed.

Kelsie turned and gave him a shove toward the door. "Put a cork in it, Millard."

TWO

"MOM, CAN I have a 'guana?" Jeffrey asked, trailing after Kelsie as she tried to get her things together for the lingerie party.

"A what?" she asked, shooing Cheevers, the striped cat, out of her tote bag. She had just enough time to get to the hostess's house in the neighboring suburb of Hopkins and get set up.

"You know, a 'guana. They're long and green and stick their tongues out."

Kelsie stopped and thought for a moment. "An *iguana*!" she exclaimed, dismayed.

"Wow! Great! Thanks, Mom!"

She snagged him by the shoulder of his football jersey before he could make a getaway. "Whoa there! An iguana is a lizard. A lizard is a reptile. You know the rule: No reptiles."

Her son looked as if she'd just told him he could never eat ice cream again. "But, Mom! Brent has one, and it's so awesome!"

Kelsie gave him a look that said don't give me any nonsense while she dug in her purse for her keys. "It's a snake with legs. No, you may not have one."

She bent and kissed his cheek. "I'll be home around eleven. Please behave yourself and don't fight with your sister."

She almost made it to the door before the phone rang.

Jeffrey grabbed up the receiver from the phone on the entry table. "Connors residence, Jeffrey Connors speaking. Shoot man, it's your quarter." He looked up at his mother's exasperated face as he listened to the caller. "Miss *Who?* Who wants to know?"

Kelsie rolled her eyes. Jeffrey was his father's

son when it came to etiquette. She clamped a hand over the mouth of the receiver as he handed it to her. "Who is it?"

He made a face as he wandered toward the couch. "Some night guy."

Alec waited on the other end of the line, a little bewildered. He certainly hadn't been expecting a little boy to answer *Miss* Kelsie Connors's phone. Another bit of intrigue to add to the puzzle of who the lady with the sexy eyebrows was. He'd spent most of his afternoon thinking about her. There was a chemistry between them that deserved exploration. She'd distracted him from thoughts of Vicious Vena, distracted him from work. And she'd seemed interested in him. At least she had until that chimp had made a monkey out of him and he'd totally blown his cool.

After that little scene she probably thought he was a jerk. She probably thought he hated animals. A rude jerk who hated animals. A dog kicker.

He hung his head.

"Kelsie Connors."

"Kelsie," he said in his satin voice, instantly

composed and confident, "this is Alec McKnight. Did I catch you at a bad time?"

Her heart pounding, Kelsie glanced at her watch. She was five minutes late. "No, not at all." Not if it meant getting another shot at the Van Bryant campaign.

"I just wanted to apologize for this morning. I lost my temper. It was very unprofessional of me."

Kelsie smiled a crooked little smile. "A chimpanzee threw coffee in your face. I think you have every right to be angry. By the way, send the cleaning bill to me, and I'll have Millard take care of it."

"Don't worry about it."

"I'm the one who should apologize—for Darwin's behavior. He never acts up. I really don't know what came over him."

"Probably spending too much time with his owner," Alec muttered to himself, compulsively straightening the items on the coffee table in front of him.

"What's that?" Kelsie asked, leaning back

against the wall, noting absently that her living room resembled an abandoned war zone.

"Ah—probably eating too much sugar. Listen, Kelsie," he began, tugging on his earlobe, a habit he'd had ever since he'd been persuaded to give up thumb-sucking when he was four. "I was wondering if we could maybe get together—"

"Sure!" He was going to give them a second chance! Kelsie looked heavenward and mouthed a heartfelt thank-you. "I'll be certain to bring the right briefcase this time. I know you'll be impressed with the work Darwin's done—"

Alec winced. "I didn't mean about the campaign. I meant you and me on a date."

Kelsie's heart shifted into overdrive. Her knees suddenly felt like marshmallows. "A date?" she asked, as if the word were only vaguely familiar to her.

"You bet." He smiled his slow, devastating smile, even though she couldn't see it.

Kelsie shivered from head to toe, then all her nerve endings went numb. If she hadn't been on such a tight schedule, she might have gotten sick. A date. A date with Alec McKnight with the million-dollar grin, holder of the fate of her business.

Just the word *date* sent Kelsie into a tailspin. She hadn't been on ten dates in the past three years. She'd dated only one man before that—her ex-husband. Mere mention of dating turned competent, capable Kelsie into a shy, insecure teenager. Since her divorce, she'd become a master at avoiding dating. It hadn't been difficult because she hadn't met anyone she was *that* attracted to. Now a man she *was* that attracted to was asking, and she was paralyzed with panic.

"Kelsie?" Alec asked. Had she hung up on him? Dead silence wasn't the usual response he got when he asked a lady out. Using his most persuasive tone of voice, he said, "Come on, Kelsie. Let me make this morning up to you. Go out with me."

Shivers coursed over her as if he'd caressed her. It took no imagination at all to conjure up the image of his direct, penetrating stare. She had to look down at the photograph of her parents that sat on the table to break the imaginary eye contact. "Um—I don't think so."

"I'm really sorry about this morning. We got off on the wrong foot. Give me another chance, Kelsie," he said, smiling to himself. He was too accomplished a bachelor not to know the effect his voice could have on a woman.

"A—gee—a—Alec," she stammered. In spite of her acute fear of dating, he was actually seducing her with his voice. Before she could succumb to the temptation, she took a deep, sustaining breath and launched into a hundred-mile-per-hour delivery of her usual rejection speech. "I'd like to but I'm afraid I don't have a lot of time for that kind of thing because between work and my kids and all I'm just really tied up and I'm already late for a lingerie party so I'd better go thanks for calling bye."

Alec stared at the phone in wide-eyed amazement. He reached down and moved it a quarter of an inch to the right on the immaculately polished antique cherry table that sat beside his smoke-blue sofa.

She'd hung up on him. She'd turned him down flat and hung up on him. Unprecedented. Still, she hadn't sounded disinterested. Nor had she said anything about seeing someone else. Talk about mixed signals!

Lingerie party, huh? Now, that sounded like something worth going to. With one finger he lifted the black satin-and-lace waist cincher he'd found behind the couch in his office after Kelsie and company had left, an idea taking shape.

"Bring on the beefcake!" Paula Budke screamed, dancing around her maid of honor's living room in a purple peignoir. Shrieks from half a dozen other partygoers egged her on as the party built to a fever pitch in anticipation of the entertainment that was to arrive shortly.

Kelsie forced a smile. She sat on the sidelines nursing a wine cooler and a vise-grip headache. Ordinarily she enjoyed these wedding showers. The women were usually in the mood for having fun and spending money. But the day had taken its toll on her fun-loving abilities. On top of everything else, she'd been fifteen minutes late to the party. The bride-to-be had been half in the bag by then.

Carla, the hostess, tossed a red feather boa around her shoulders and cranked up the stereo so that the driving, sexy beat of Prince's latest hit song rattled the glass in the china cabinet. Two of the bridesmaids danced out of a bedroom, modeling more lingerie.

Kelsie sat back and thought of Alec McKnight, reasonably certain she was going to throw up. Alec McKnight wanted to go out with her—on a date. Alec McKnight, who could have melted the polar ice cap with his smile, wanted to go out with *her*, Kelsie Connors. Alec McKnight, who at the moment, wielded a lot of power over her future.

The last thing she wanted to do was offend him, but she would not go out with him to make this deal. No matter how badly she needed to land the Van Bryant ad campaign, she wouldn't sell herself for it. Not that he had suggested such a thing; it probably hadn't even occurred to him.

He's a man, isn't he? her alter ego asked. Of course it occurred to him.

Stop it, she scolded herself, not all men were the kind of pond scum Jack turned out to be.

Regardless of his intentions, she couldn't go out with Alec McKnight. She had a business to run and another job at night. Between the two she had to sandwich in quality time with her children to be Mom *and* Dad. Then there were the two cats, the dog, the parrot, the rabbits, and fish that needed her attention too. And she had a dozen other responsibilities as an organizer for civic groups and charities. How could she even think of being wined and dined by Alec McKnight?

What did she know about dating anyway? Nothing. She'd been a bookish wallflower in high school. When Jack Connors had asked her out, she'd latched on to him like a burr on a dog. She'd come a long way since those days, but she still didn't know anything about the subtle aspects of dating. According to what she'd heard from single girlfriends and women at these Naughty Nighties parties, the dating scene was one big anxiety attack. Who needed that?

The doorbell was ringing. No one seemed to hear it but Kelsie. Big surprise, she realized. Half the wedding party was doing the cancan on the sofa, while Rod Stewart wondered in song if anyone thought he was sexy.

Sexy? Kelsie grimaced, going to the door. The guy didn't need a mask for Halloween. Alec McKnight was sexy. Alec McKnight was—

Here.

Kelsie's jaw dropped open so hard she was sure she heard it hit the floor. Alec McKnight stood in the doorway looking gorgeous in an unzipped leather bomber jacket, a cardigan sweater the exact shade of his eyes, a white shirt, and snug jeans that hugged his legs.

"Hi." He smiled, his direct stare capturing her eyes and holding them prisoner.

"Alec," she managed at last. "What on earth are you doing here?"

He lifted the black undergarment with two fingers hooked through the satin lacing. "I thought you might need this. You left it in my office," he said in a voice that suggested she had left it there after an afternoon of wild sex.

Blushing, Kelsie snatched the waist cincher away from him, unconsciously holding it against herself as if to judge for size. Alec's mouth started to water as he imagined what she'd look like wearing the provocative garment. She wasn't very curvy but had a sleek, subtle figure, the kind a man's hands could slide over with no difficulty, he thought as he surveyed the soft rose-colored blouse and snug-fitting navy blue skirt she wore.

"How did you find me?" she asked, having to nearly shout as the volume of the party rose behind her.

"I called your house. Your daughter told me where you were," he shouted, his dark brows drawing together as he looked beyond Kelsie to the wild scene in the living room.

There were unmentionables everywhere. Scraps of silk and satin and lace were draped over furniture and hanging from the chandelier. Six nearly nude women were doing the cha-cha around a tray of hors d'oeuvres. "What the hell is going on here?"

Before Kelsie could begin to explain, a blood-curdling scream split the air. *"He's here!"*

Suddenly Alec was yanked into the room, into a sea of shrieking women. They danced around him, bumping and grinding, exuberantly singing along with the Beatles on "Twist and Shout."

"Hey!" he yelled, trying to jump back from a blonde in yellow silk pajamas who started unbuttoning his shirt. He backed into a buxom redhead who was stealing his jacket but managed to duck away from a brunette who was eying his jeans.

In the background, women were clapping and chanting, "Take if off, Studs! Take it off, Studs!"

Kelsie pinched the bridge of her nose and closed her eyes for a second, shaking her head. Just when she'd thought the day couldn't get any worse, these women had to mistake Alec McKnight for Studs Malone, male stripper extraordinaire.

"Ladies! Ladies!" she shouted, trying to wade through the gyrating bodies to rescue poor Alec. He didn't stand a chance against a bevy of bachelorettes. Neither did anyone trying to save him. By the time Kelsie had fought her way to him, she'd lost the combs out of her hair, three buttons off her blouse, and part of a sleeve.

Alec looked like he'd been rolled by a gang of thugs. His hair was disheveled and his shirttail hung out of his jeans. His shirt gaped open to reveal a sculpted chest lightly dusted with dark curls. Carla had thrown the red boa around his neck. The bride had him by the belt and was doing the twist. Kelsie tried to shoulder her aside.

"He's not Studs Malone!" she yelled, hooking a finger through a belt loop on Alec's jeans to steady herself.

"Who cares!" Paula exclaimed. "He's a hunk!"

It was then that the real Studs Malone walked in, dressed head to toe in skintight black leather for his Wild West act. He was none too pleased to see another man stealing the limelight. Ignoring the women tearing at his cowboy outfit, he stormed toward Alec. Kelsie had gotten pushed away, but when she saw the glower on Studs's face, she redoubled her efforts to get to Alec.

"Who the hell are you?" Studs demanded, hands resting on the butts of his white pearl-handled six-guns.

"Alec McKnight," Alec answered, torn between relief at seeing someone of his own gender and apprehension at the look on the guy's face. "Brother, am I glad—"

"What do you think you're doing, horning in on my gig?" Studs clamped his Stetson down low over his eyes, looking like he was about to say "Draw, pardner."

Stunned that anyone could think he'd purposely subject himself to a strip search by a bunch of crazed women, Alec could only gape at Studs. Studs somehow took that the wrong way, and, just as Kelsie arrived on the scene, he took a swing at Alec.

The punch caught her a glancing blow off her left cheekbone, but Kelsie went down for the count like a felled prize fighter, dropping back into Alec's arms as the police stepped into the house.

When she started to come around, the first thing Kelsie saw was a blurry, somewhat one-dimensional image of Alec McKnight. He was bending over her with a worried expression creasing his forehead and turning down the corners of his interesting mouth. In the foggy recesses of her mind, she wondered what that mouth would feel like on hers. It was finely chiseled, with an almost cynical twist to it when he wasn't smiling. Yet it wasn't hard-looking. It looked kissable.

As things came more into focus, she could see beyond Alec to two uniformed police officers. Police officers? She tried to sit up, groaning at the sudden bass drum beat in her head.

"Easy, honey," Alec said in a soothing voice, stroking a hand down the side of her face. Luckily it was the side that didn't feel like it had been kicked in by a Clydesdale. His fingertips were firm and warm.

"What happened?" she said, moaning, levering herself up on her elbows. Alec helped her sit up on the couch, positioning himself beside her so he could get a good look at her.

"Jeez," said the taller cop with the thinning blond hair, "you got socked by a guy in a leather cowboy suit."

"For real?" Kelsie asked. Her memory was too fuzzy at the moment for her to trust it.

"I think so," the cop said, nibbling on a cheese puff from the hors d'oeuvres tray, "but you never can tell nowadays. They make a pretty good vinyl that looks just like the real thing."

Not following his answer at all, Kelsie groaned and looked around the room. The party was over. Evidently one of the neighbors had called the police because of the noise. Many of the women had left for home. Paula, the bride-to-be, was dozing in a recliner, snoring loudly, with lingerie piled across her a foot deep.

"How long was I out?" Kelsie asked.

"Just a few minutes," Alec said, fingering the purplish bruise that was beginning to color her left cheekbone, wincing when she winced. "He didn't hit you very hard."

"Oh, really?" she said dryly. Her head felt as if it had been used for a soccer ball.

"But you're going to have a shiner," he added.

"Piece of raw meat's the best thing for that," said the tall cop.

The cop with the bad toupee shook his head. "Cold bag of cheese curds. Conforms better to the shape of your face."

The pair wandered away discussing the relative merits of cheese curds.

"Kelsie, I feel terrible," Alec said, looking boyishly contrite.

"That makes two of us."

"That punch was meant for me." What was she going to think of him now, he wondered. That he was a rude jerk who hated animals and let women take his punches? Obviously he was going to have to postpone asking her out.

It seemed to Kelsie that who Studs meant to punch was irrelevant now. She was the one with the blackening eye. At any rate, the whole thing had been nothing more than a huge misunderstanding.

"What happened to Studs?" she asked one of the officers.

"Some other cops hauled him away. Do you want to press charges?"

"No," she said, resting her throbbing head in her hands. "I want to go home."

Alec insisted on driving her. He even talked the policemen into following them with Kelsie's battered Blazer so she wouldn't have to return for it the next day.

She huddled against the door on the passenger side of his car, trying to hold her head up on her shoulders, a task that seemed not unlike balancing a bowling ball on a thumbtack.

"I had no idea those lingerie parties got so wild," Alec said, piloting his car down the dark, quiet streets of Hopkins toward the suburb of Eden Prairie, where Kelsie lived. "How long have you been selling?"

"Three years. Since my divorce." Now, why had she mentioned that, she wondered. Before he could jump on the opportunity to make personal conversation, she rushed on. "They usually don't get this crazy, but I went to one in Bloomington once that was raided by a church group. It was pretty exciting, because the minister's wife was modeling a pair of baby doll pajamas when they stormed in."

"Divorced three years with two kids to raise. Must be kind of tough."

"I manage." If he wanted the gory details, he was going to have to resort to torture. She wasn't going to discuss her private life with him even if there were very tempting notes of empathy and sympathy in his voice. She didn't want to get into any deep conversations with Alec McKnight, conversations about things like why he had driven to Hopkins to deliver something he could have stuck in the mail. In fact, she decided, the less she said the better. If she kept her mouth shut, he couldn't very well talk her into going out with him—that was assuming he was still interested in her after all that had happened.

So she didn't want to talk about her divorce, Alec mused. He could relate to that. Maybe once they knew each other better, they could swap horror stories. *If* she allowed them to get to know each other better, he added silently.

"How long have you had Monkey Business going?"

"Two years."

"Do you enjoy it?"

"Very much."

"It must be interesting work."

"Yes, very."

The car rolled to a halt at a red light. In the soft glow of the dashboard lights, Alec turned a slow grin on Kelsie that had her wanting to turn down the car's heater. "Are you ever going to answer me with more than two words?"

"Probably not," she said, fighting a smile in spite of her headache. She stared down at her feet, afraid if she went on looking at him she would keel over on the seat.

He kept his smile firmly in place as the car pulled away from the intersection. "Are you going to go out with me tomorrow night?"

Kelsie's breath bolted out of her. Her one good eye widened in surprise. "I don't think so," she managed to say.

"That was more than two words," he pointed out with a chuckle. He wasn't terribly put out by her rejection. She wasn't refusing because she wasn't interested. He knew chemistry when he saw it and felt it. She just needed some coaxing. "I was hoping for 'I am.'"

"I can't."

"Close, but no cigar," Alec said, pulling up in front of her house.

"It's nothing personal, Alec," she explained. "I just don't have the time to date."

They got out of the car as the tall policeman drove up in Kelsie's Blazer with his partner following behind in the squad car. Still holding one hand to her throbbing head, Kelsie glanced up and down the street, hoping none of her neighbors happened to be looking out their windows. Her menagerie hadn't exactly endeared her to a couple of them. She hated to think what they'd say if they saw her coming home at midnight with a police escort.

She and Alec both thanked the officers for being so accommodating.

"No problem," Officer Johnson, the taller one, said.

"You bet," said Officer Baines, grinning. "It's kinda nice to have something weird break up a guy's shift."

After the police had driven away, Alec walked Kelsie to the front door.

"Don't take this the wrong way, Kelsie," he said, huddling into his bomber jacket as they stood under her front porch light. His breath silvered the October night air. "But you seem to have a real knack for being at the center of bizarre situations. I've hardly known you for a day, and I've been assaulted by a chimpanzee and mistaken for a male stripper."

"Those kinds of things don't usually happen to you?" she asked, straight-faced.

He looked down at her and chuckled. Her hair was mussed all around her head, and even in the poor light he could see her left eye blackening. She was so appealing, he thought—and she was nervous about standing out there on the porch with him and no chaperone except the trio of jack-o'-lanterns on the steps.

He wasn't used to women being nervous around him, but he thought it was probably a very good sign. Or a very bad sign. There was only one sure way he could think of to find out.

"You're really something, Kelsie Connors," he murmured, sliding the gloved fingers of one hand over her hair to cup the back of her head as he lowered his mouth to hers.

Kelsie would have backed away from him if the doorknob hadn't been jabbing her in the back. The idea of kissing Alec McKnight scared her silly. In the first place, she hardly knew him, but, more important, it frightened her because she *wanted* to kiss him—*really* wanted to kiss him. The ramifications that kind of wanting could have on her already hectic life made her shake all over.

She's shivering, Alec thought as he settled his mouth ever so gently against her lips, lips that were even softer than they looked. He drew her against him, sharing his warmth while the kiss lasted.

Kelsie leaned into him, her hands clutching the waistband of his jacket. For just a few sweet seconds she forgot her fear and indulged herself in the pleasure of a simple good-night kiss. His mouth was warm and pliable and tasted a little like cherry candy. He smelled like leather and musk aftershave, and he felt good against her. Too good.

"Um—a—" she stammered as he raised his head. "I'd better go in and see if I can find some cheese curds for my eye. Do you think it would matter if they were lightly breaded?"

"Probably not." Alec grinned, flashing his dimples at her inane prattle.

"Good." She turned, fumbling with her keys, and let herself in. She stood in the doorway, feeling a little safer. "Thanks again for the ride."

"You're welcome," he said, his gaze holding hers in that way of his that made her so nervous.

"I'm really sorry about all the confusion."

"It's okay. Don't worry about it. It's kind of nice to have something weird happen to break up a guy's evening," he said.

"Right." She tried to laugh. "Good night." She started to back into the house, but a thought occurred to her, and she poked her head back out the door. "This didn't count as a date, did it?"

Alec shook his head, smiling as he hopped down to the sidewalk and started walking toward his car. Her door clicked shut behind him. He licked the sweet taste of her from his lips. "Mmm. We'll start counting next time, Kelsie. And there will be a next time."

THREE

"KELSIE, IT'S BUCK. I need a weasel first thing Monday."

Kelsie sandwiched the receiver between her shoulder and ear as she jotted down notes with one hand and spun the wheel of her Rolodex with the other. "Does it have to be a weasel? I don't think I have a weasel. I can get you a ferret."

"Is that like a weasel?"

"Sort of. What's it for?"

"A magazine ad for farm insurance," the

photographer said. " 'Weasel in the Henhouse' is the theme of the thing."

"A fox in the henhouse," she corrected him. "A fox is what you need, Buck," she said, turning to the name of a small game farm in Waconia that had several hand-raised foxes. "A fox will photograph better anyway—all that bright red hair, bushy tail."

"You're right. I don't know what I was thinking. What's a fox going to set me back?"

"Fifty an hour. Two-hour minimum."

Once the details had been discussed, Kelsie hung up the phone and sat back in her squeaky desk chair, pressing a half-thawed bag of spinach to her eye. Her desk, a rummage-sale reject, was piled with files: a pile of animal-client files, a pile of files of past customers for animal talent, a pile of sale coupons for dog and cat food, and a pile of bills.

Even though it was Saturday, she had every intention of sorting through the entire depressing mess. If Glendenning wasn't going to use Darwin for the Van Bryant ads, she was going to have to redouble her efforts to find work for her other clients, or she was going to find herself in financial hot water.

Kelsie had faith in her business. She knew there was a market for animal talent, not only in advertising, but for live appearances as well. What Monkey Business needed was more exposure. But exposure meant advertising, and advertising meant spending money, big money. It was one of the frustrating catch-22s of operating a small business: She could make more money if she advertised more, but she couldn't afford to advertise until she made more money.

She groaned in frustration, squeezing the mushy spinach into a better position against her swollen cheek and eye as she listened to a load of clothes tumble in the drier in the corner behind her. She stared at the little cartoon pinned to the corkboard on the wall above her desk. A chubby little cat proclaimed nothing would happen today that couldn't be cured with a large dose of chocolate. At that moment she'd have given anything for a big, thick square of pure, unadulterated fudge.

Cheevers bounded onto her desk and curled up

to sleep on the stack of bills, ignoring Kelsie with the supreme arrogance of a cat. Kelsie regarded him through her good eye. If she could get Cheevers another ad for Seafood Sam's, she would make enough to buy a couple of spots on the radio for the upcoming holiday party season. She would have to check into it Monday.

Jeffrey came down the cellar steps in his pajama bottoms and a rumpled Twins World Series sweatshirt, rubbing his eyes, his thick blond hair standing on end. Without a word he shuffled to his mother's desk and leaned against her.

Kelsie hugged him with one arm. "Morning, buster."

"Mmm. How come you're holding that green slime on your eye?"

"It's spinach. We didn't have any cheese curds."

"Huh?" He laid his cheek atop her head.

"I had a little accident last night and hurt my eye. Nothing major."

"Did somebody clobber you?" he asked with more enthusiasm than concern.

Kelsie pushed her chair back from the desk. "Let's go make some waffles."

When it came to diverting her son's attention, food was infallible. Jack had been the same. Jeff was like his father in so many ways, it was almost frightening. At nine years old he was already showing signs of having Jack's sturdy frame and unmanageable hair. Kelsie said a little prayer daily that the similarity would end there.

The doorbell rang as they reached the kitchen. Kelsie sent her son to see if his sister was awake and went to the door herself, expecting to see the paper boy waiting for his payment. But when she swung the door open, still holding the bag of spinach to her eye, instead of finding the freckle-faced boy, she found a full-grown man.

"Alec!" she said with a gasp, her heart slamming against her ribs.

Alec took deadly aim and hit her right between the eyes with the most devastating smile he could conjure up. "Morning, Kelsie," he said in his best morning-after voice, even though there hadn't been much of a night before. Leaning negligently against the doorframe, he handed her her morning paper.

"Aren't you a little old for a paper route?" she asked, not able to think of anything more intelligent to say. It was a wonder she could think at all with Alec McKnight standing on her doorstep in a black sweatshirt and jewel-blue sweat pants, his hair comfortably mussed, his lean cheeks flushed from the chill of the morning.

"Just helping out," he said. "I happened to be running by—"

"You live around here?" she asked, feeling all quivery inside at the thought that Alec McKnight could be her neighbor.

He grinned. "No. I decided I needed a change of scenery for my morning run."

His gaze ran over her with all the speed of molasses in January, taking in every detail, from the haphazard part in her hair, to the old Vikings jersey that subtly revealed the fact that she wasn't wearing a bra, to the skintight black knit pants that hugged her slender legs like tights, to the rag wool socks that bagged around her ankles. "And believe me," he said, "this is the best scenery I've seen in a long time."

As his low, silky voice slid over her in an intimate caress, Kelsie shivered even though she suddenly felt flushed with fever. Her breasts tingled and tightened, her nipples budding against the fabric of her jersey as if Alec had reached out a finger and brushed it against them. The mere thought brought a heavy rush of sensation to other parts of her that had almost forgotten what pleasure a man's touch could bring.

She was way out of her league with Alec McKnight. He was obviously an *nth*-degree black belt in the swinging-singles game. It was like going up against a lion armed with a toothpick.

"How's the eye?" he asked, mercifully straying from more provocative topics for the moment.

"Sore." A slight understatement. Even after a dose of mega-strength aspirin it hurt worse than it looked. She couldn't imagine why Alec had been eating her up with his eyes the way he had. She'd glanced in the mirror earlier just long enough to decide she looked like a poster girl for a battered-women's shelter.

"What's that you're holding against it?" he asked, poking cautiously at the bag with a finger.

"Chopped spinach. It was the best thing I could find. I know it looks terrible, but I look even worse without it. I hadn't planned on seeing anyone today. Any time you look better with a bag of chopped spinach plastered to your face than without it, you shouldn't let yourself be seen by anyone outside your immediate family."

With gentle fingers Alec peeled the bag away from her face and examined the swollen, bruised cheekbone. "It doesn't look so bad," he murmured.

"Well," Kelsie said, her eyes locked on the sensual curve of his lower lip, which was only inches away. "I suppose it's nothing a pound of makeup wouldn't hide."

His forefinger trailed down her cheek and tipped up her chin as he leaned a little closer. One good deep breath from either of them and their mouths would have been drawn together, Kelsie thought, little jets of panic and anticipation zipping through her.

"How about inviting me in for a glass of orange juice?" he whispered as if it were a terribly intimate suggestion. Directions to the Metrodome would have sounded suggestive in the tone of voice he was using.

Kelsie was about to offer him everything in her refrigerator and then some, when an old red pickup truck pulled up to the curb in front of her house and a dozen floppy-eared, brown spotted Nubian goats leapt out onto her lawn.

"Oh, wow, goats!" Jeffrey exclaimed, pushing through the doorway past Kelsie and Alec. "Can I keep one?"

A short, round man in bib overalls and a cap that advertised a seed corn company came around the back of the truck and waved, a pleasant smile on his face as if he didn't realize he'd just set loose a dozen four-legged lawn mowers in a neighborhood where the residents weren't particularly fond of farm animals. "Morning, Miss Connors!"

"Mr. Svenson," Kelsie said with a groan, trotting down the steps. "Didn't I tell you I'd call if I found any jobs for your goats?" So far the little creatures seemed to be content grazing on her frosty lawn, while Jeffrey wandered through their ranks in his stocking feet, trying to pick out the one he liked best. Kelsie kept one eye on them, waiting for the inevitable disaster.

"Well," Mr. Svenson said as he rubbed the first of his double chins. "I thought you might have forgotten about me."

"Never." Kelsie tried to smile as a little goat braced its front feet against her thigh and began to nibble at the hem of her jersey. Next door, her sour-faced neighbor, Mrs. Magruder, was peering out her living room window, glaring at Kelsie. "Goats just aren't in demand right now. I *will* call you if I find something, though."

Mr. Svenson frowned at Alec, who had come down to stand next to Kelsie with hands on his hips and a bemused look on his face. "It's a conspiracy, you know," the farmer said. "That blasted dairy association. They're anti-goat. Always have been."

Alec nodded, trying to look grave. A big brown goat with a bell around its neck stared up at him, then proceeded to try to eat the ends off his shoelaces.

"You see," Mr. Svenson said, warming to his

subject, "cows eat a heck of a lot more. Makes a bigger market for hay and whatnot—"

A booming bark cut the lecture short. Bronco bounded around the corner of the house. Suddenly goats were bolting everywhere, and the dog was dashing around the yard, enjoying his game immensely.

"Oh, no!" Kelsie wailed as three goats sailed into Mrs. Magruder's yard, one landing smack in the middle of a bed of yellow mums. Another scaled the woman's front steps and balanced itself on a decorative cement mushroom beside the door. "Jeffrey, grab Bronco!"

The boy made a dive for the dog but missed. Kelsie, Alec, and Mr. Svenson all dashed onto the lawn to try to round up the goats. Mrs. Magruder stormed onto her front step in her bathrobe with her pug dog hanging over her arm, the dog yapping. Mrs. Magruder glared at Kelsie from beneath a cap of pink curlers. She was a retired schoolteacher whose husband spent all his time at the local Moose Lodge. Her lawn was her pride and joy, and she'd disliked Kelsie from the day they'd met, when Kelsie's cat, Cheevers, had beat up the Magruder's ugly pug.

"I have half a mind to call the police!" she yelled. "I have half a mind to call Councilman Reid!"

"You've got half a mind all right," Kelsie muttered under her breath. "E.T. wouldn't have a dog that ugly." To Mrs. Magruder she said, "Really, I'm very sorry, Mrs. Magruder. I'll fix everything."

Back in her own yard things were finally getting under control. Jeffrey struggled up to her with a goat in his arms. "Mom, can I keep this one?"

"No," Kelsie answered. "Put it in the truck with the others."

"Sorry about the commotion, Miss Connors," Mr. Svenson said, loading the last of his herd. "They're not used to dogs. If that had been a sheep, they wouldn't have even noticed."

Kelsie glanced at Bronco, who was dragging Alec toward the backyard. He might have passed for a small pony, but not a sheep. "I'll call you if anything comes up, Mr. Svenson. Maybe there will be a better market for goats around Christmas."

"You could be right about that," the farmer said, climbing into his truck.

Kelsie took a deep breath as the pickup drove away and her son trudged back to the house.

"Well, that was certainly something I don't do every day," Alec said, brushing dirt off his clothes as he crossed the yard toward Kelsie.

Poor Alec, Kelsie thought. He couldn't get within fifty feet of her without having something bizarre happen. "Thanks for helping, Alec."

"Don't mention it," he said, plucking a blade of grass off his tongue.

They both sat down on the front steps and sighed.

"So, what are you doing tonight?" Alec asked. If he was lucky, she would be feeling worn down enough by now to concede and simply answer "going out with you."

"Dishes, laundry, and the bathroom tile," she said. If she was lucky, that answer would turn him off enough to discourage him from pursuing her. Of course, most men would no doubt have given in after the chimpanzee incident, or the stripper incident. Being confronted by a herd of dairy goats surely should have done it. Yet here he was, asking her out.

She had to hope he would give up soon—before she grew too used to looking at him. It was just so obvious to her that there was no room in her life for an affair with a man like Alec McKnight, or any other kind of man for that matter. How could it not be obvious to Alec as well? Hadn't he seen enough?

Alec watched her worrying her soft lower lip with her teeth, obviously hoping he'd take the hint and back off. Not a chance, Kelsie, he thought, determination rising in him. "How about this afternoon?"

"Work, bills, raking, repairing goat damage to Mrs. Magruder's yard, and laundry."

"You said laundry twice."

"I have a teenage daughter and a nine-year-old son; of course I said laundry twice."

Did she really keep such a hellish schedule, he wondered. "When do you take a little time for Kelsie Connors?" he asked softly, his gaze searching hers for an answer she seemed unwilling to give.

"Every year I take off three hours to watch the rerun of *The Sound of Music,*" she said, unreasonably annoyed at his probing. Why wouldn't he just leave her alone instead of adding another problem to her already complicated life? "Alec, I wasn't putting you off when I said I don't date. I don't date. I don't have the time or the energy for it. I have too many things to do to go out with you tonight or any other night." She pushed herself to her feet.

Jeffrey stuck his head out the door. "Mom, when are we gonna eat? I'm *starving!*"

"I'll be there in a minute. Go make yourself a piece of toast."

Alec stood up, dusting off the seat of his sweat pants. "I'd better be going."

Kelsie ran a hand through her tangled hair and sighed. "Look, I'm sorry I took your head off, Alec. My temper's running on a short fuse today." Probably because she'd spent the whole night alternatingly dreaming erotic dreams about him and worrying about how not to have a relationship with him without ruining her slim chance to do business with Glendenning. "Would you like to stay for breakfast? I owe you that much for helping with the goats."

Alec shook his head, his mind busy working on the puzzle that was Kelsie Connors. "No, thanks," he said absently. "I have some things to do this morning. I'll see you later."

"Bye," she said, disgusted with herself for feeling so sad as she watched him walk away. He might call her again, but she doubted she'd see him. It seemed she had been successful in discouraging him. Why didn't that make her happy?

She had turned him down yet again. A sensible man would have thrown in the towel right then and there, Alec told himself as he walked the ten blocks to where he'd parked his car. Why waste time chasing a woman who wasn't interested? Because she was interested. He'd seen it in her eyes, in the way she blushed when he smiled at her. Dammit, he'd tasted it in her kiss!

Was she playing some kind of game with him?

If he decided to reconsider using her client in the Van Bryant campaign, would she suddenly find the time to go out with him?

He wouldn't do that. He would not compromise his professional integrity to get a date even if she did have the sexiest eyebrows in the upper Midwest.

Alec slid behind the wheel of his BMW, disgusted with his cynical train of thought. Not every woman wanted to use him as a rung on the professional ladder, he reminded himself. He should be ashamed for being so suspicious. Kelsie Connors was as far removed from Vena DiMarlo as Minnesota was from Mars.

Of course, he had reason to be suspicious, he thought as he started the car and headed north toward the suburb of Minnetonka. He could remember with painful clarity how completely Vena had fooled him. She'd seen him coming a mile away—a generous guy in a position to get her a big break in modeling, a guy with a decided weakness for lovely ladies in need.

McKnight in shining armor, he thought and scowled.

Vena had taken gross advantage of his weakness, using him to get her break. Personally he thought she'd missed her calling. She was the consummate actress. But modeling was less work. That was Vena; she took as much as she could get for the least amount of effort.

At least she hadn't managed to totally corrupt his attitude toward women. He was wiser, warier, but he was no misogynist. He hadn't been tempted into any long-term relationship since Vena, but that was because he was enjoying his second chance at bachelorhood. He was enjoying keeping his own schedule, keeping his town house the way he liked it—immaculate—he liked going out when he wanted and with whom he wanted.

Which brought him back to Kelsie Connors. His attraction to her had been instantaneous, and it has grown stronger despite her seeming reluctance—or, perhaps, because of it. Whichever it was, he certainly wasn't going to let it stand in his way, he thought, grinning as he drove toward home.

There were three things Alec McKnight had never been able to resist: A mystery, a challenge, and a pretty lady in distress. Kelsie Connors qualified on all counts. He'd find a way to get around her "no dating" rule, and he'd be doing her a favor. By the sound of things, she needed rescuing, and he was just the McKnight for the job.

Back in Eden Prairie, Kelsie pulled another waffle out of the iron and scolded herself for thinking about Alec. If he'd ridden up the front steps on a white charger, she couldn't have gone out with him. She was just too busy.

"Mom? Mom. *Mom!*" Elizabeth finally yanked on her mother's sleeve. "You're waffling a potholder!"

"What?" Kelsie snapped out of her trance.

Black smoke rolled out of the waffle iron. With a little gasp she pulled the thing open and peeled the smoldering potholder off the iron with a fork.

One more thing to add to her list of things to do. One more reason to add to her list of reasons she couldn't go out with Alec McKnight. She had to clean the melted fabric shreds out of the waffle iron.

Heaving a sigh, she slid down on her chair and stared at her waffle. She had no appetite for it. The only thing she would have considered appetizing was a pound of Fanny Farmer chocolates. Or Godiva chocolates. Or a big stack of plain Hershey bars. A waffle held no magic for her this morning. The only thing that made her gag it down was the thought of how much it had cost to make it. Bisquick didn't grow on trees. There was probably a penny's worth of electricity spent, too, and a new potholder would set her back a buck and a half. It all added up.

She watched Jeff sop up half a quart of syrup with his waffle. He ate with great enthusiasm, savoring every spongy little square, pausing only to gulp down some milk every so often. Elizabeth, on the other hand, had picked her breakfast apart until it resembled a pile of crumbled foam rubber.

"Are you going to eat that or just torment it some more?" Kelsie asked.

Elizabeth took a guilty bite and said nothing.

"You'd better get a move on if you're going to be ready to go by the time your dad gets here."

"*If* he gets here," Elizabeth muttered, earning herself a furious glare from her mother.

Kelsie glanced at her son. Jeffrey was busy sneaking toast crusts to the cats under the table.

Neither of her children had any illusions about their father. They knew Jack was undependable, that he took little or no interest in their lives most of the time. But Jeffrey still had hope. He wanted very badly for his father to love him and want him and want to do all the father-son things other kids' dads did. It would never happen, Kelsie knew, but she didn't have the heart to burst Jeffrey's bubble. It was like letting him believe in Santa Claus. Sooner or later he would find out for himself, and she'd be there to help ease the hurt. In the meantime, it was the unwritten rule that Elizabeth not make derogatory remarks about Jack in front of her brother.

"I'm not going," Elizabeth said more loudly.

Jeffrey's head popped up above the table again. "Come on, Lizbeth, it'll be neat. Dad said we're gonna help him look for deer tracks in the woods so he'll know where to go hunting." He stared at his sister with his big brown eyes filled with a certain kind of vulnerability, as if he were afraid his sister's defection would somehow jinx the rare afternoon with their father.

Elizabeth wouldn't meet his gaze. "Julie asked me to go to the mall with her. You go with Dad and have a good time."

"We will," he replied in a tone of voice that was meant to convince himself as much as the others.

Jack was late, as usual. Every time it happened, Kelsie told herself that the next time she wouldn't waste the energy it took to be furious with him, but she never held herself to it. Every time she ended up replaying their dismal failure of a marriage over in her memory while she waited for him to show up.

He'd been cocky and self-assured when she'd married him. They had both been too young. She had believed he would channel that cockiness into something positive, that it would grow into pride and invite respect as he worked his way up in his father's contracting business. Instead, it had grown into overbearing arrogance.

In her more philosophical moments, Kelsie thought it was sad that such a bright young man had turned out to be so detestable. He was going to end up lonely, with an empty life. Today was not one of those philsophical days, however. She mentally called him every name she could think of as she sat on the couch going through her files and watching her son pretend to play with Transformers on the living room floor as he waited with one hopeful eye trained on the picture window.

Finally a maroon Corvette pulled up at the curb. Jeffrey was out the door and down the sidewalk in a flash.

She deserved a chocolate fix after this morning, Kelsie decided, leaning back against the storm door as her ex-husband drove away with their son. It had been a long time since she'd given in to her compulsion. She'd been proud of her self-control, but a person could take only so much. Her limit had been reached. Now she could almost taste the chocolate. She sighed in resignation and ran a hand through her already mussed hair as a black BMW pulled up to the curb.

A boy of about fifteen with spiky brown hair

climbed out of the backseat. From the front passenger seat emerged a small, dark-haired older woman wearing a white sweatshirt with the words CLEAN AND MEAN stamped in black across the front. Probably relatives of one of the neighbors, Kelsie thought, straightening to open her door. Then the car's driver emerged.

With wind-riffled dark hair.

And to-die-for blue eyes.

And a grin that could have helped him sell snowmobiles to desert nomads.

Alec McKnight rounded the hood of his car, his gaze locked on Kelsie's. She felt all her energy drain right down from the top of her head to her feet, as if someone had just poured a bucket of warm water over her. Sweet heaven, he'd stopped grinning, and she was still losing control. He was thinking about smiling, though, she could tell, and that was almost as bad. The idea played and tugged at his lips, teasing her mercilessly.

He seemed to be getting more handsome every time she saw him, she thought, feeling dazed and amazed. Old jeans hugged him in all the most interesting places. He wore battered sneakers and a sapphire-blue sweatshirt. Boundless, restless energy carried him across her lawn with the long, unconsciously elegant stride of a dancer.

Oddly it was the first time Kelsie had taken much notice of his build. He was six feet tall, no more; lean but athletic-looking with square shoulders that stopped short of being wide. Then his smile flashed, bright and brilliant, and Kelsie was incapable of noticing anything else.

"Hi," he said, stopping at the bottom of the steps.

One syllable. Those eyes, that smile, and just one syllable combined in a way that suggested intimacy. With one word he could make a woman feel as if she'd shared the night with him.

Kelsie groaned under her breath. She had to break eye contact or run the risk of promising him anything. She hadn't expected to see him again, but he was here, and she felt such a soaring joy inside that it terrified her.

"Hi," she said, glancing away, her gaze falling on the two people rummaging through the trunk of Alec's car. "What are you doing here, Alec?"

"I'm here to rescue you." Grinning, he swung an arm in the direction of the car. "I've brought reinforcements. Alice is taking the house, Miles is taking the lawn, and I am taking you out tonight."

FOUR

"ALEC!" KELSIE SAID with a gasp, pressing her body back against the storm door. "You can't bring a cleaning lady in here; my house is a mess!"

Alec's straight dark brows knitted together in confusion. "Kelsie, that's what cleaning ladies do. There wouldn't be much point in bringing a cleaning lady over if your house was already clean."

"Men!" Kelsie muttered under her breath. Their minds seemed to have a completely foreign mode of operation. "I haven't had time to do any kind of housework for a week. What is this woman going to think of me?"

Alec shook his head and smiled. "She'll think you're a lady with two jobs and two kids to take care of. It's not as if she's never come into a household in that situation before. It's not as if she's going to think you're a slob or anything."

He peeled Kelsie away from the door and let himself in, mentally eating his words. A basket of laundry had been dumped on the couch in the living room. Some kind of dangerous-looking electronic monsters were scattered on the floor. A messy stack of stuffed manila file folders was piled on a coffee table thick with dust. There were five pair of shoes abandoned behind a recliner in front of him and a mound of Naughty Nighties lingerie on the seat of an old rocker across the room. Near the TV a small magazine rack had been overturned.

Trying to overcome the sudden dizziness the sight of a horrendous mess always brought on, Alec leaned back against a table cluttered with mail. A gray cat bolted from under the far end of the table, upending a sorry-looking potted plant. Dirt scattered across the tan carpet as the plant keeled over. From its cage in the dining room, an enormous blue parrot shrieked and said, "Damn!"

Kelsie could have died of embarrassment, not so much because of the state of her house—her house was usually a mess—but because Alec was seeing it. Only very good friends and door-to-door salespeople saw her house in its natural state. Alec didn't fall into either category.

Just what category did he fit in, Kelsie asked herself. *Dangerous* was the word that came to mind, though she wasn't certain why. Just because he wanted to go out with her didn't make him a candidate for the ten-most-wanted list.

How about the *one*-most-wanted list?

Before she could blush at the thought, she forced herself to wonder where he found so many clothes that exactly matched the incredible deep blue shade of his eyes. Did he choose them for that reason, or was it unconscious?

"Alice Bigelow," came a voice from beside her.

Kelsie looked down at the woman, startled and

dismayed. She wished a hole would magically appear that she could disappear into, but smiled valiantly. "Kelsie Connors."

"Nice to meet you," Alice said, coming farther into the room armed with a bucket full of the tools of her trade. She held up a bowl brush as she headed down the hall. "I like to start with the bathroom."

"Alec," Kelsie said under her breath. "I can't believe you brought a cleaning woman to my house. You hardly know me."

"I'm sorry," he said pleasantly, having recovered from his initial shock. "I know that's something most guys don't try until the third or fourth date, but I was afraid we wouldn't even have a *first* date—"

"You got that right," she said, bending down to right her ailing dieffenbachia. She scooped dirt off the carpet and patted it around the base of the plant. "I can't go out with you, Alec."

"Ah!" He held up one finger. "You said you were too busy to go out with me. If all your housework gets done, you won't be too busy."

She gave him a smug look as she shoved the

pile of shoes under the recliner. "I still can't go out with you. My daughter has a babysitting job tonight, and my son isn't old enough to stay home alone."

Alec shrugged. "So get a sitter."

"Ha! That shows how much you know." Kelsie shook her head as she rounded up Jeffrey's Transformers. "It is a proven fact that babysitters cannot be had for a Saturday night with less than forty-eight hours' notice."

He frowned. "They're that hard to come by?"

"They're practically on the endangered species list." Even as she told him this, her traitorous mind was rattling off options. Jeff could spend the evening with their neighbor, Thor, who loved kids. Or he could possibly stay with his best friend, Brent, if Brent's mother didn't mind.

Alec briefly considered the possibility of taking Kelsie's son along, but dismissed it. The company of a nine-year-old boy was not likely to make for a fun date. He wanted Kelsie all to himself anyway.

She thought she'd won the battle. He could see it in her eyes. Kelsie was just going to have to learn Alec McKnight did not give up easily. He'd been described as having the determination and drive of a bulldozer, qualities he never hesitated to use—supplemented with a generous dose of charm—to get what he wanted.

"Can I use your phone?" he asked, trying to look perfectly innocent.

"Sure. It's somewhere behind you, under the mail." Kelsie tipped up the magazine rack, stuffing three months' worth of magazines into it, keeping one eye on Alec as he made his call.

He really wasn't handsome, she thought, contradicting her earlier impression. He was . . . appealing . . . interesting . . . dangerous. There was that word again. The sunlight coming through the picture window fell on his dark brown hair, bringing out deep red highlights.

"Hello, Natalie?" He grinned, looking down, absently sorting Kelsie's mail into neat stacks. Kelsie had the fanciful idea as she watched him that his flash of white teeth could affect a woman even over the phone lines. "It's your dear, devoted cousin, Alec. Remember that *huge* favor you owe me?"

Kelsie's jaw dropped. He was getting a baby-sitter! *Now* what was she supposed to do?

Before he could ask the big question, she dashed across the room and made a grab for the phone. With two fingers, Alec lifted the chunky white instrument out of her reach as he returned the smug look she'd shot him moments before.

Disgusted, Kelsie leaned back against the brown tweed recliner, glowering at Alec as he made the arrangements for his cousin to sit with Jeffrey for the evening. When he hung up, she asked, "Did it ever occur to you that I just may not want to go out with you?"

Alec shook his head as he advanced on her, his gaze holding her motionless as a smile made his lips twitch. "Nope," he said, corralling her against the chair with an arm on either side of her. "Not once. But then, I'm an optimist. Can you look me in the eye and tell me you really don't want to go out with me?"

Was that supposed to be a joke? She could hardly look into his direct, warm, blue velvet gaze without promising she'd follow him to the ends of the earth! And, darn him, he knew it. He was using his best asset to an unfair advantage. She wanted to wipe that charming smile off his face by denying any attraction to him, but, when it came right down to it, she couldn't.

"You don't play fair," she muttered.

Alec gave her a slow, Cheshire cat smile. "How do you feel about Chinese?"

She swallowed hard as she glanced down. His body was deliciously close to pressing against hers. How many times in the past two days had she felt her own body reacting to this man's nearness? More than was safe to recall.

"Chinese?" she echoed. "As a language or a cuisine?"

"Ouch! Ouch, ouch, ouch!" Kelsie winced as she gingerly applied makeup to the discolored area around her left eye. "How's this look, honey?" she asked her son, who stood scowling in the bathroom doorway.

"Looks like a black eye with a lot of goop on it."

Kelsie checked the mirror again. He was right.

She hadn't managed to hide the problem, and if she added another layer of cover-up, she was going to look like a geisha girl. Disgusted, she grabbed a tissue and started wiping the stuff off. "Ouch! Ouch, ouch, ouch!"

"Why don't you just stay home?" Jeff suggested.

Kelsie felt a stab of guilt at her son's remark. It wasn't the first stab of guilt she'd felt since she'd given in to Alec's dinner invitation, and it wouldn't be the last. With her workweeks so hectic, she always made a special effort to save time on the weekends for the kids. She especially tried to spend time with Jeff after an outing with his father, because he often came home moody.

She tossed her tissue into the trash and bent over to kiss her son's cheek. "I'm sorry, sweetheart. I can't get out of this."

Liar, her conscience responded, you don't *want* to get out of this.

"What do you say to renting that *Star Trek* movie tomorrow night, and we'll have a little party of our own?"

He shrugged, still frowning. "Can we have pizza?"

"You're having pizza tonight."

"Can we have it again?"

"We'll see," she said, returning to the mirror above the vanity to give her cheeks a quick dusting of blusher.

As far as she was concerned, she looked like death and felt very near it. She was cold all over, shaking, and her stomach was in knots. Lord, how she hated the idea of dating. It was almost a phobia. No, it *was* a phobia. In any ordinary business or social situation she could meet a man, have a normal conversation, be reasonably charming, but label that situation with the word *date* and she was reduced to a quivering, babbling, pathetic shell of a person.

"And they say war is hell," she muttered to herself, fumbling with the thin black ribbon tie at the throat of her blouse.

It probably had something to do with her upbringing. She'd grown up on a farm, with only her little sister Danielle for company. Their nearest neighbor had been a mile away and no one in the area had had children Kelsie's age. She'd grown up terribly shy and a little insecure, making her sister and her pets her best friends. Boys had seemed alien to her. Somehow, the concept of dating brought all those old feelings back to her.

"Can I get a tarantula?" Jeffrey asked, sensing this might be the time to get his mother to agree to what she might otherwise think were unreasonable demands. Before she could reply, the doorbell rang. He dashed off to answer it.

He swung the door open and glowered up at Alec. "Who are you?" he demanded, hands on hips, barring the entrance to the house as best he could.

Alec looked down at the boy, knowing instantly he had his work cut out to win over this little ruffian. He held out his hand, thinking the manly gesture might break the ice. "I'm Alec McKnight. I helped with the goats this morning."

"So?" Jeff said, ignoring the offered hand.

Alec stuck his hand in his pocket, clearing his throat. He looked at his cousin Natalie and raised his brows. "This is Natalie. She's going to stay with you while your mom and I go out."

Jeff glared at the pretty, dark-haired young woman. "I don't need a sitter."

"Gee, I guess not; you're a big guy," Natalie said, unperturbed. "But I'm here, so would you mind if I just stayed? I've got a lot of studying to do. I'm a law student."

The boy looked her up and down, considering, obviously leaning toward saying no.

"I brought fudge ripple ice cream."

"Okay." Jeff nodded, motioning her in. "I'll show you where to put it." He headed for the kitchen with Natalie behind him.

Cheeks pink, Kelsie emerged from the hall with a wry smile. "My son the pit bull. I'm sorry, Alec."

Alec shrugged it off. "You look great."

She had tamed her blond hair back into a pony-tail and wore a snug black wool skirt and a roomy tan blouse with narrow black vertical stripes. A black ribbon was tied in a bow at her throat. Letting his eyes roam back down to her skirt, he noted she had great legs—long and shapely and breathtakingly sexy in dark, silky stockings. He wondered if she was also wearing any of those delicious little underthings she sold. He'd had the most erotic dream about her showing up at his office wearing nothing but the black waist cincher he'd found behind his couch.

"Thanks," she mumbled, her eyes darting all around the room. She tried to get a look at him without making eye contact. That was the secret to saving herself. Eye contact was the key to his high-powered magnetism. She caught a glimpse of a black and gray print casual shirt, dark gray pleated trousers, a stylish pair of shoes, Cheevers getting ready to pounce—she scooped up the fat orange cat, holding him away from her body so he wouldn't shed on her. "Sorry. He was about to leap on your shoe. He has a thing for feet. Jeffrey! Come and get Cheevers!" She paused, watching Alec sneeze repeatedly into a monogrammed handkerchief. "Are you all right?" she asked.

"Fine." He managed to smile as his eyes watered. Jeffrey gave him a derisive look as he slung the cat over his shoulder and retreated to the kitchen. "Just a little allergy. I can't get within three feet of a cat."

Kelsie frowned. She abruptly ducked, calling,

"Kitty, kitty, kitty." With no sign of a cat forth-coming, she straightened and tried to smile at Alec's bewildered look. "My other cat likes to hide under the library table. I didn't want him to sneak up on you."

He was saved from having to comment when Natalie entered the room. After the introductions had been made, Kelsie started for the kitchen to show Natalie where key items were located, leaving her son and her date eyeing each other.

"Jeff, why don't you show Pirate to Mr. Mc-Knight?" she called over her shoulder.

Jeffrey made a disgusted face and motioned Alec to follow him to the dining room, where a macaw that had to be three feet long to the tip of its tail feathers perched inside an antique-looking cage in one corner of the room. The bird was cobalt blue with a strip of yellow under its jaw, and unblinking brown eyes.

"That's Pirate," Jeffrey said flatly. He stuck his hands in the pockets of his jeans and looked as bored as was humanly possible.

"Is he tame?" Alec asked, hoping to generate

some sort of conversation that would last until Kelsie came back.

"Sure," Jeff said, glancing at the bird to hide the shrewd look that had come into his eyes. He reached into a drawer in the oak buffet that sat along the back wall of the room. "Here, you can feed him a palm nut..." he said, handing the nut to Alec.

Alec held the palm nut between two fingers. He slipped them gingerly inside the cage. The parrot shrieked and bit him.

"Ouch!" he yelled, biting his tongue on the string of curses that were ready to tumble out. He yanked his hand back from the cage and sucked on his wounded finger.

"But he might bite you," Jeffrey finished with an angelic look.

"What in the world?" Kelsie said, coming into the room, wondering what all the commotion was about.

"It's nothing, really," Alec said, giving Jeffrey a hard stare. "Your parrot doesn't like me."

"He doesn't like strangers," she said. "Hyacinth macaws are like that. Jeffrey, you should have warned Mr. McKnight that Pirate doesn't like strangers."

"I'm sorry, Mr. McKnight," he said, gazing sincerely up at Alec.

It was weird, Alec reflected as he and Kelsie sat at a corner table in a Chinese restaurant, what lengths he seemed willing to go to just for a date with this lady. His cleaning woman was going to be able to retire to the South of France on what she'd charged him for cleaning Kelsie's house. His eyes were still itching from the close encounter with the cat. His finger had gone numb where the parrot had bitten him. Then there was the little incident with the male stripper, not to mention the goats. He should've known he was in for trouble after the monkey fiasco.

None of that seemed to matter. He still wanted to take Kelsie Connors out—on a regular basis, if nothing worse happened to him. It wasn't only because she was a lovely lady and he was a man with a healthy libido. He got the impression she didn't give herself many opportunities to have fun as a woman—not as somebody's mom or some-body's agent or somebody's lingerie lady, but as a woman—and it made him sad. She deserved more out of life than working herself into the ground. It was unaccountably important to him that she should get more out of life.

She sat across from him, fidgeting and biting her lip. She looked as nervous as a teenager—a look that did funny things to his heart—and she had been rattling on nonstop about the most bizarre subjects ever since the waitress had taken their order and left them alone.

"... And, you see, it's almost impossible to tell a female spotted hyena from a male, because they all have the same markings, so the females appear to be males."

Alec thought he deserved a medal for keeping a straight face. She sounded so serious. It had to have been nearly twenty years since he'd seen a girl so nervous on a date. "That must keep things interesting in the old hyena den," he said. "Is that why they're always laughing?"

"What?" Kelsie asked blankly. She'd suddenly

forgotten what she'd been babbling about. Alec had to think she was a world-class idiot by now.

"Laughing. Laughing hyenas."

"Oh. Yeah." Why did she have to be such a dismal failure at this? She was an intelligent person. She was a competent mother and business person. Why did she have to act like all her brain cells had gone south now?

"How's the eye feeling?"

"Better than it looks," she said.

"I really don't think the dark glasses are necessary," he suggested gently. "People are staring."

"Great," she said. "They'll really stare if I take them off. They'll think you beat me up."

"Maybe," he agreed, taking a sip of tea. "Or maybe they'll think you were in a car accident or that you got hit playing racquetball or—"

"Or got popped by a male stripper."

"In an all-leather cowboy outfit." He smiled warmly, coaxing an answering smile out of Kelsie. She slipped the sunglasses off and stuck them in her purse.

"Why are you so nervous?" he asked point-blank, curiosity lighting his eyes.

Kelsie considered denying it as she eyed the couple across from them, but figured it was so obvious there was no point. "I'm not very good at this," she said shyly.

"What? Going out to dinner?" he asked. "You don't have to use the chopsticks, you know."

"Dating. I'm not very good at it."

"I have a feeling you don't get enough practice. Why is that? You're an attractive, appealing woman. Why don't you give yourself a break once in a while, Kelsie?"

His question stung. Probably because it poked too close to the truth—truths she knew about and some she wasn't willing to examine. A surge of defensive anger vaporized her jitters. "Look, Alec, I'm not fishing for pity or anything here, but I think you need to understand things that aren't that simple when you're trying to raise two kids and keep a business from going under."

Alec stiffened a little. Watching for her reaction very carefully, he said, "Your business isn't doing very well?"

Kelsie played with her silverware, wishing

she'd kept her mouth shut. "Things could be better."

A thread of tension tightened between them and tightened a little more when he said, "If, for instance, I reconsidered on the Van Bryant deal."

Kelsie's head shot up, her eyes not avoiding his now. Her heart beat a little faster. She couldn't have been that wrong about him, could she? "Is that one of the perks I get for going out with you, Alec?" she asked with deadly quiet.

"Did you think it would be?" he returned.

"For the record, no," she said, seething inside. How dare he think that of her? He'd practically dragged her to this damned restaurant, and yet he had the utter gall... She pushed her chair back from the table and started to get up to leave. "Thanks for the lovely evening."

"Kelsie, wait." Half out of his chair, Alec caught her wrist, thinking he more than deserved the glare she shot him. "I'm sorry. I think we both hit a nerve. Truce, okay?"

Kelsie sat just as the waitress brought their dinners. After the woman had arranged the plates of steaming, wonderful-smelling food on the table, she left them alone.

"I'm sorry," Kelsie said, poking a fork at her almond chicken. "I told you, I'm not very good at this dating stuff."

"It's simple," he said, digging into his beef with broccoli. "We make small talk, have a nice dinner, we go back to my place, and you let me ravish you."

Kelsie almost choked. The look on her face was one of pale, wide-eyed panic.

Alec had to laugh. "Honey, I'm teasing," he assured her. Not that he didn't want to take her back to his place and ravish her. His imagination had been going wild on that particular topic practically since the moment he'd met her.

Kelsie sighed in relief and tried to ignore the tiny nip of disappointment inside her. It had been so long, she wasn't sure she remembered how to be ravished, but there was little doubt in her mind that Alec could give her a top quality refresher course. She struggled to push the thought out of her mind and remember she was just having dinner with him, not a relationship.

"Where'd you go to college?" he asked, effectively ending both their forays into fantasy.

"I didn't."

Alec's brows bobbed up in surprise. "I figured you had to have a degree in zoology. Where did you learn so much about animals?"

She grinned. "*Wild Kingdom.* I never missed an episode as a kid. *National Geographic* specials too."

"Why didn't you pursue it?"

Kelsie hesitated. She almost said fear, which would have been a large part of the truth. The idea of leaving her safe, closed environment for college had terrified her then. Instead, she gave her stock answer. "I got married. We started our family right away. I used to think about going to college, but I don't anymore. I like what I'm doing. How about you? What's your story, Alec?"

"Pretty boring stuff." He smiled. "Born and raised in Edina, a business degree from the University of Minnesota, went to work at Glendenning. I live in Minnetonka and like to run every morning."

"Aren't you awfully young to be a vice-president?"

"I'm ambitious, and determined—remember that." He gave her a wink.

"Do you have family in the area?" she asked, feeling remarkably relaxed now that her initial nervousness had passed. They were sharing a lovely meal and conversation; there was nothing scary about it.

Alec nodded. "My dad still practices law downtown. Mom has a little needlecraft store. I have some aunts and uncles and assorted cousins scattered around. You?"

"My father sold the farm and retired last year. He and Mother are living in New Mexico. I have a younger sister, Danielle, who is part-owner of a salvage shop in Chicago."

The rest of the dinner passed pleasantly enough. Kelsie had calmed down to the point where she could actually taste and appreciate the subtle flavors of the food. Alec ate because there was a plate in front of him. He was too wrapped up watching Kelsie and appreciating her subleties to care about the cuisine.

She had totally captivated his interest. He was by nature a curious person, and Kelsie was like a very pretty puzzle to him. She had seemed so nervous at the start of the evening, one might have thought she'd never been on a date, yet she had been married and had two children. She had told him she didn't date because she didn't have time, but he had sensed there was more to it than that. She struck him as being intelligent and self-sufficient. She had a job that required her to get out and hustle for business, yet she could seem almost painfully shy.

He was intrigued, which meant one thing at present: This wasn't going to be their only date. He wanted to get to know Kelsie, wanted to be the one to rescue her from her self-imposed life of work and more work. She might not think she needed or wanted rescuing, but that wasn't going to stop him.

"What's your fortune?" he asked. The waitress had left their cookies and gone off to retrieve Alec's change from the bill.

Kelsie cracked her cookie open, plucked out the slip of paper and read it, making a face.

"Strength of character through virtue and hardship."

"They gave you the wrong cookie," Alec said, teasing. "I told them to give you the one that said 'A long and happy life through unbridled lust.'"

Kelsie rolled her eyes and tossed her fortune at him. "What's yours say?"

Alec read the message to himself, a slow grin spreading over his face as if he was a poker player who had just laid down an unbeatable hand. "Good things are coming to you in due course. Perseverance rewards itself."

The night was clear and cool when they left the restaurant, with a moon well on its way to being full hanging in the sky. Kelsie huddled into her light coat and caught herself wishing Alec's arm were around her as they crossed the parking lot to his car. The thought surprised her. Not because she was fantasizing about him again—she'd been doing that since they'd met—but because she wasn't nearly as uncomfortable with him as she had been only a few hours before.

Their dinner conversation had hardly been of the deep, soul-searching variety, and it had put her at ease. He was a nice man. He hadn't loaded the conversation with leading remarks or come-ons. They had talked like two mature adults getting to know each other. It seemed a simple thing, but loomed large in Kelsie's mind, considering how it had changed her attitude.

Driving out of the parking lot, Alec went straight instead of turning in the direction of Eden Prairie and Kelsie's house. She shot him a suspicious glance.

"Where are you taking me, Mr. McKnight?" she asked in her mother's don't-give-me-any-bull tone of voice.

"For a drive around the lake," he answered innocently, fighting back a grin. "It's a beautiful night, don't you think?"

"Lovely."

"It's probably been a while since you went for a quiet moonlit drive around the lake."

"A while." The last moonlit drive around a lake she'd taken had been when Jeffrey was a baby with a brand of insomnia that could only be cured by taking him for a ride in the car. It had hardly been a romantic experience.

"So I'm treating you to a moonlit drive around the lake."

"Fine, but don't get any ideas, McKnight," she warned.

Alec chuckled. "Too late for that."

They drove around the night-silvered lake in companionable silence with light rock music playing softly on the car's stereo. When they came to a parking lot near a strip of beach, Alec turned into it and killed the engine.

"Don't ask me how long it's been since I've parked with a man," Kelsie said with humor in her voice.

Grinning, Alec slid across the seat and put his arm around her shoulder. "How long has it been since you've parked?"

"I think Nixon was president." They both laughed.

"Then it's been too long," Alec declared, lowering his mouth to hers for a slow, sweet kiss.

It didn't matter that she'd nearly forgotten how to kiss a man; she let Alec lead, and it seemed he'd been born to do just that. His mouth moved on hers, gentle and coaxing, rewarding her with a low groan as she allowed his tongue access to the warmth beyond her lips.

Alec shifted on the seat, trying to position them both so he could pull her against him, a move he had mastered in his teenage days that eluded him now. He settled for changing the angle of the kiss and running his fingertips into the baby-soft tendrils of hair that hadn't made it into her ponytail. He kissed the corners of her mouth, her chin, the tip of her nose, the eyebrows he found so irresistibly sexy, then pulled back a bit to gauge her reaction.

She was undecided. Not about Alec's talent at kissing. She was undecided as to whether or not she should allow herself to fully enjoy it. It seemed like it could quickly become addictive. Then, too, her lack of experience haunted her. What was she supposed to allow him on this first date? What was he expecting, and what would he think if she gave more or less? She could still remember when kissing on the first date had been considered scandalous.

"You'd better not try getting me in the backseat, buster," she warned.

Alec laughed and gave her a quick kiss. Her uncertainty and that hint of vulnerability in her eyes made her a refreshing change from the women he'd been dating since Vena. Everything about Kelsie was unique and fascinating to him.

She glanced over her shoulder and out the window. "I keep expecting to see officers Baines and Johnson peering in at us."

"We're out of their jurisdiction," he said, running a forefinger down the short slope of her nose.

"Yeah, but they just might be out looking for something weird to break up their shift."

Their shared laughter mingled with the latest tune from Bruce Hornsby singing through the speakers.

Alec leaned back against the seat, smiled, and shook his head as he recalled the wild events of the night before. "I will never forget that experience as long as I live. It was kind of fun."

Kelsie groaned. "Speak for yourself. You didn't get kayoed by Black Bart."

"Aw, poor sweetheart." He leaned over and touched the lightest of kisses to her black eye. "Does it hurt?"

"Only when I squint."

"I'll make it up to you. Let's go to my place for dessert." He had to laugh at the look she gave him. "Dessert, honest, it's not a line. I promise not to ravish you. I make a hot fudge sundae that'll knock your socks off."

"Never say hot fudge to a chocoholic." She moaned.

"You're a chocoholic?"

"Confirmed and incurable."

"Mmm. You shouldn't have let me know your weakness, Kelsie. I will take full and unfair advantage of that if need be."

She scowled at him. "You're ruthless."

"You bet. How about that sundae?" He smiled, bobbing his eyebrows.

Regret and guilt collided in Kelsie's stomach. She wished she could say yes, felt guilty that she wished she could say yes, felt guilty about Jeffrey being home with a sitter, felt regret at knowing her evening with Alec was almost over, regret that it could be no more than an evening.

For form's sake, she checked her watch. Her sigh was genuine. "I can't, Alec. I really should get home. I need to spend a little time with Jeffrey before he goes to bed tonight. He's had a rough day."

Alec bit his lip to keep from saying something imprudent. He was actually feeling jealous of a nine-year-old boy, he realized, thoroughly ashamed of himself. He had to remember Kelsie's sense of responsibility. He had had to move heaven and earth just to get her to go out to dinner with him; it probably wouldn't be wise to push for more. Not this time.

"Okay," he said, forcing the corners of his mouth up. "Next time we go for the sundae."

"Alec—" Kelsie began.

He turned to her, pressing a forefinger to her lips. "Don't tell me there isn't going to be a next time. Did you have fun with me tonight?"

She nodded, trying to concentrate on the conversation instead of on the way he touched her.

"I had fun too." He smiled gently. "And we can

have fun together again. There's no law against Kelsie Connors going out for a little fun once in a while."

No, she thought as he drove her home. The danger was in making a habit of it.

FIVE

"YES, FOLKS, IT's a zoo at Big Olie's Car Carnival this weekend!" shouted a portly man wearing a safari suit and standing next to a zebra. He puffed on a huge cigar, stared into the television camera, and continued. "Come on down! Bring the kids! Free popcorn! Free elephant rides! Everything's free except the cars!"

The zebra sat down as the commercial came to an end.

"Blasted striped jackass," Big Olie, the car salesman, muttered.

The zebra's handler took the reins and coaxed the animal to stand, as Kelsie stepped forward. "Big Olie, I think the radio remote people want you in the showroom with the myna bird," she said, gasping for air in the cloud of his cigar smoke.

"Have that camel ready for the next TV spot," he ordered, waddling off across the car lot.

"It's a llama," Kelsie said, stroking the zebra's nose, knowing the man neither heard nor cared.

She rubbed at the start of a headache in her temples as she asked the handler to show the zebra to the hundred or so kids waiting none too patiently in line by the service department. The young man Neillson's Petting Zoo had sent to handle Ubu the llama assured her he would have the animal ready and in place by the time Big Olie came back.

Kelsie leaned back against a late model sedan out of the customer flow and tried to catch her breath. She'd been working without a break since six-thirty in the morning, coordinating the "zoo" for Big Olie's sale. Big Olie was an exceedingly un-pleasant man to do business with, but he'd hired a dozen animals for the entire day, which made all the aggravation worth the prize-winning headache she felt coming on.

"Kelsie, we need some help over here with the lion!"

"Be right there!" she called back.

"Kelsie, where do they want the kangaroo?"

"Has anyone seen the scoop shovel?"

"Has anyone seen the boa constrictor?"

Kelsie closed her eyes. "I'd sell my soul for a Snickers and five uninterrupted minutes to eat it," she whispered to herself.

Another thing that was adding to her headache was the fact that in spite of being run ragged and having twenty people pulling her in twenty different directions all at once, she still couldn't keep thoughts of Alec from creeping into her mind.

He'd called three times during the week to try to talk her into going out with him. She'd refused each time, citing perfectly legitimate reasons why she couldn't see him. The joke was, she did see him. She saw him every time she closed her eyes. She saw him in her dreams.

What was this foolishness going to get her?

Nothing but heartache. Despite what Alec said, she didn't believe they could have even a casual relationship. No matter how determined he was, he couldn't change the fact that she had responsibilities that took up all of her time.

Even if she could somehow finagle more free time to go out with him, what would come of it? She doubted Alec had given much thought to the reality that he wouldn't be getting involved only with her, but also with her children and an extended family of animals. They were a package deal. Once he realized that, would he still be interested? When he decided no, who would be the one to get hurt? She would, and she didn't have time for a broken heart.

One corner of her mind refused to listen to reason, however, and it was driving her crazy. How many times in the last week had she told herself it was futile to attempt to have a relationship with Alec?—hundreds, at least. Yet there he was when she closed her eyes, his face indelibly stamped on her memory: his dark hair with its subtle highlights of red, the high cheekbones, the blue eyes with their disturbing, intent gaze, the interesting, expressive mouth with its wide, perfectly symmetrical smile and the dimples that flanked it.

With a weary sigh Kelsie opened her eyes to banish the image. It didn't go away. She blinked twice before she realized it was no figment of her imagination. Alec stood in front of her with his hands in the pockets of his leather jacket, the breeze lifting his hair. He smiled at her, and, as if by magic, produced two candy bars on one outstretched palm. She looked up into eyes the color of serenity— deep, calm blue. A wave of warmth washed over her. "Alec, is it really you or am I hallucinating?"

His dimples winked at her as he flashed her a grin. "It's really me. Are you saying I'm the man of your dreams?"

"I'm saying this day has been the stuff nightmares are made of. I wasn't so sure my mind hadn't just conjured up a knight in shining armor to rescue me."

"That happens to be my latest calling," he said. "I'll have my white charger brought around and we can ride off into the sunset."

Didn't she just wish? Standing there in shrink-to-fit jeans and a red sweater, the breeze feathering back his dark hair and mischief sparkling in his eyes, he looked ripe for running away with.

As she looked up at him, a rare thing happened. She suddenly felt completely, utterly overwhelmed. Kelsie Connors, who always had to be strong for everyone else, suddenly wanted to lean on someone. She wanted to lean on Alec, could easily imagine what it would feel like to have him put his arms around her and tell her everything would be all right. It was a scary feeling to want to let the responsibility fall on someone else, when she knew it was hers to shoulder.

"We knights in shining armor thrive on this kind of thing. Didn't you know that?" he asked, glancing around at the chaos of Big Olie's parking lot.

Kelsie shook her head. "I've never had a knight at my disposal before. I don't know how to behave at all."

That wily, dangerously male smile rode his lips as he looked down into her eyes. "There you go again, Kelsie, telling me things I can take gross advantage of."

"I thought knights had a code of honor." She smiled sweetly.

"I thought you didn't know anything about knights," he said, letting his head drop down a little nearer hers so he was no more than a whisper away from kissing her.

Without even thinking about it, she moistened her lips in anticipation. Alec smiled and took a step back from her, removing the delicious threat of intimacy for the moment.

"I spoke to your daughter on the telephone and she told me where you were and what you were going through. I thought you might enjoy a little pick-me-up," he said, holding out the candy bars and chuckling at the desperate look she cast at the treat he'd brought her. "Let's find a moderately quiet corner and enjoy these together."

As usual, he'd made a perfectly innocent suggestion sound like arrangements for a lovers' tryst. Kelsie groaned at that thought and the knowledge that she didn't have time to eat four heavenly inches of chocolate and caramel. "I can't, Alec. I'm going nuts trying to keep all this under control."

"Why don't you let someone else be in control for a few minutes?" he suggested, pocketing the candy and stepping closer again. He settled his hands on her waist and tried to drop a kiss on her lips but hit her cheek when she turned suddenly.

"Kelsie!" a voice shouted. "Someone has to come hold Randolph; I drank too much coffee this morning!"

Kelsie managed a weary smile as the rest of the zoo crew laughed. "See what I mean?" she said to Alec, squirming out of his grasp, almost glad for the distraction. His hands felt too darn good on her body.

"I can lend a hand," he offered, following her down a row of cars, weaving through prospective victims of Big Olie's hard-sell routine. "Just tell me what to do."

That was the whole idea of his McKnight in Shining Armor campaign, wasn't it? To help make life a little easier for Kelsie. He could certainly hang on to a leash of a chimpanzee or something. He didn't have to know anything about animals to do that.

"I don't know, Alec," Kelsie said. "Randolph is

a cat. What about your allergy?" She turned at the end of the row of cars and kneeled down. "Hi, Randolph. How ya doin'?"

"Oh, my lord!" Alec gasped, freezing in his tracks. "Kelsie, that's a *lion*!"

"Of course he's a lion."

He watched in horror as she rubbed her cheek against the big cat's head, her hands buried in the thick tawny mane. Every gruesome story he'd ever heard about models and actresses getting mauled by lions, every safari movie he'd ever seen came back to him in vivid Technicolor. "For crying out loud, don't get so close!"

Kelsie laughed and ruffled the lion's mane. "Don't worry. He doesn't have a tooth in his head. He'd be about a hundred years old if he were a human."

Alec heaved a relieved sigh and backed away a step as his eyes began to itch and water.

"Maybe we'll name our new cat after you, you big lug," Kelsie told the lion.

"New cat?" Alec asked with a noticeable lack of enthusiasm.

Kelsie nodded. "I volunteer a day a week at our

local animal shelter. This week someone left the most adorable little fawn-colored kitten. Poor little thing, he looks like someone's kids decided he needed a haircut and they did the honors with dull sewing shears."

"So, naturally, you had to bring him home," Alec concluded.

"He looked so lost, Alec. It just broke my heart."

The look on Kelsie's face was so irresistibly sweet, all Alec could do was make a mental note to call an allergist first thing Monday and make an appointment to get himself cat-proofed.

"What time will you be finished here?" he asked. "I thought we could grab a bite to eat afterward, maybe see a movie."

"Oh, Alec," Kelsie said with a sigh. Was he never going to give up? Did she really want him to? "When I finish here, the only thing I'm going to want to see is a bathtub and a bed."

"Sounds great," he said in the intimate way that made all her nerve endings sizzle. His lips turned up at the corners with the promise of a sexy smile. "Your place or mine?"

She felt weak as she imagined sharing a bathtub with Alec. She could remember from their first kiss how lean and hard his body was. It seemed only natural to speculate on what he looked like without clothes. Did he have tan lines? These and several more questions brought a blush to her cheeks, as if she thought he could read her mind with his penetrating gaze.

As Randolph's handler returned, someone else called for Kelsie. She stood up, dusting off her khaki slacks, craning her head to see around the people in the car lot. "Oh, no, here comes Big Olie. It must be time for the llama spot."

"Kelsie!" Someone called from the other direction. "I need a break, or I'm quitting!"

Kelsie ground her teeth. "Alec, if you really want to help, go relieve the guy with Gumby."

"What's Gumby?" Alec called after her as she strode toward the area where two local television stations had trucks set up to do live coverage of the gala event. Suddenly a long, bony hand covered with stringy red hair clamped down on his shoulder. Slowly he turned to face a very unfriendly looking orangutan. "You must be Gumby."

Big Olie lit a fat green cigar and took the llama's lead line from Kelsie.

"I don't know if it's wise to smoke around him, Big Olie," she said with a worried frown, swallowing hard to keep from choking on the noxious fumes. "Llamas are very sensitive creatures."

Big Olie snorted and scowled at her. "This cigar is my trademark, sweet cheeks. I don't give a rip if this camel doesn't like it."

"Okay, fine." Kelsie sighed, lifting her hands in defeat and stepping back as the cameramen prepared to start shooting.

"Big Olie here from Big Olie's Car Carnival on Crosstown," he began, puffing a cloud of greenish smoke around his head and Ubu's. The llama blinked its huge brown eyes in surprise and raised its head ever so slightly. "It's a zoo here at Big Olie's today! Free—oh—"

"Cut sound! Cut sound!" one of the TV crew shouted frantically as Big Olie let loose a string of curses that would have put a sailor to shame.

Kelsie rushed forward to grab Ubu's lead before the llama could bolt away from the man he'd spit all over.

"Get that stupid camel out of my face!" Olie shouted. Someone tossed him a towel, which he rubbed furiously over the front of his safari suit. "Get that monkey over here!"

Kelsie handed the llama over to one of her helpers and looked frantically around for Gumby.

"N-n-nice G-G-Gumby," Alec stuttered as the orangutan shook him by the shoulders like a rag doll.

"Alec," she called. "Please stop playing with the orangutan and bring him over here!"

She was becoming an obsession. Alec didn't care. After a week of seeing what an ungodly schedule she maintained, he was more set than ever on rescuing her. Obviously she'd missed the chapter in the history book about Lincoln abolishing slavery. She'd probably been out working when the teacher had covered it.

It wasn't just work. Alec reflected as he made his bed with military precision, then padded naked across the polished hardwood floor to his walk-in closet. He understood the hours she had to spend working and the time she wanted to spend with her children, but it seemed there wasn't a committee in Eden Prairie she wasn't a member of. The PTA, the Cub Scouts, the figure-skating club, the youth hockey mothers, the Humane Society, the League of Businesswomen, the garden club, the Daughters of Scandia. The list seemed endless.

"And ridiculous," he grumbled as he selected a pair of jeans from the section of the closet where all his slacks hung in neat groups—dress slacks, casual slacks, dress jeans, old jeans. He pulled a blue plaid flannel shirt from the casual shirt group, then picked up a gray sweatshirt from the cubicle where he stored them and his crew-neck sweaters. He snatched up a pair of sneakers from the neat row of shoes on the floor.

It was as if she had to be all things to all people. Supermom syndrome, that's what it was, he decided. Well, being a supermom was all well and good, Alec thought, but what was going to become of the part of Kelsie that wasn't a mom? What about her needs as a woman?

"That," Alec said to his reflection in the mirror after he had dressed, "is where I come in, Kelsie."

Sunday. It was supposed to be a day of rest, wasn't it? Kelsie asked herself as she laced on a pair of figure skates. She was dog tired from the long day she'd put in at Big Olie's, but she'd promised the kids a day at the ice arena to brush up on their skills before their respective seasons of hockey and figure skating began. So she laced on her skates and daydreamed about spending the day soaking in a tub of bubbles, where the water never got cold and she never dropped her book in and the phone never rang and none of the cats came in to stare at her as she bathed.

A long hot bath. A long hot bath with Alec McKnight.

Blast, she thought as heat rose in her cheeks despite the less than toasty temperature in the skating rink, why could she not stop thinking about him?

"Come on, Mom!" Jeffrey called as he zoomed past, weaving through the other skaters making their way around the rink at various speeds. Several, like Jeff, seemed bent on setting new speed-skating records and scaring the devil out of the less accomplished skaters. Others moved at a more leisurely pace, enjoying the piped-in waltz music and the rhythmic motion of skating in time to it. Elizabeth was at the center of the ice practicing spins. Then there were the beginners, who had obviously decided to try to master the basic skills before winter came and the rinks got crowded.

Kelsie carefully made her way onto the ice, then gasped. Across the rink a man who looked amazingly like Alec was struggling along through the crowd. It was Alec! "What are you doing here?" she asked when he'd caught up with her.

"Enjoying myself immensely," he said. "We'd better move before we get run over." He was teetering precariously. "I haven't been on skates since I was twelve," he said. "How about helping me get the hang of it again?"

Kelsie tugged at the collar of her turtleneck as Alec's smile warmed her. The effect he had on her body's responses was unlike anything she'd ever encountered. That knowledge, along with the realization that she really did want to have a relationship with him, coupled to double the sense of panic welling up inside her. She swallowed hard, pushing the sensation back down to her stomach.

"If you haven't been on skates in all that time, why are you here today?" she asked.

He let his gaze caress her before he answered. "Because you are."

Her involuntary little gasp delighted him. Every response she gave him was encouragement. He took it and her arm with a grin and tried to scoot far enough away from the rink boards to get going. They made their way around the ice in fits and starts. Every time it seemed Alec was getting his balance and rhythm back, he would suddenly find himself struggling to remain on his feet. It didn't help that he and Kelsie laughed hard enough to fall over every time it happened either.

After three grueling trips around the rink, Alec begged for a breather. He followed Kelsie off the ice and collapsed onto a bench beside her. His legs felt like sprung springs. It was an unpleasant surprise to discover that the muscles he toned and hardened every morning running along Lake Minnetonka were apparently not the same muscles he needed to ice-skate.

"Mom, can I get a Coke?" Elizabeth asked, stepping through the gate from the ice to the locker area. She was out of breath, her cheeks flushed from the exertion of practicing spins and jumps. Her long blond braid hung down over one shoulder, blocking out part of the pattern of her soft blue ski sweater. She wore heavy blue tights and a bouncy fuchsia skating skirt.

"Sure, sweetheart. My purse is in the locker. Let me get the key out of my pocket," Kelsie said, lifting her hips off the bench so she could get her hand into the pocket of her faded jeans.

"I've got change," Alec said, digging into his own pocket more to distract himself from Kelsie's squirming hips than anything else.

Elizabeth gave him a curious look, then glanced at her mother.

"Elizabeth, this is Alec McKnight, a friend of mine," Kelsie said, curious to see her daughter's reaction. Elizabeth's eyes widened into two huge blue pools.

"We've spoken on the phone," Alec said, handing the girl change for the pop machine. He gave her his most charming smile as well. "I'd stand up, but I'm not too steady on these things. It's nice to meet you, Elizabeth."

"Oh..." was all she managed to say. "A—um— it's nice to meet you too. Thanks for the change," she stammered, and retreated to the Coke machine.

"Pretty girl," Alec commented softly, his eyes on Kelsie's face. "Takes after her mother, I'd say."

"Thank you." She smiled shyly, looking down at her skates. "I think she was impressed with you too."

"You think so?" With cool, gentle fingers he tipped her chin up and turned her face toward his. "Have I managed to impress her mother in the least?" he asked quietly, letting his fingertips roam over her face, tracing the shape of her dark, sexy eyebrows, the contours of her rosy cheeks, the outline of her daintily sculptured upper lip and its full, soft counterpart.

Kelsie's heart raced and her breath became shallow, as if Alec's tantalizing touch were somehow robbing the oxygen from her. All she managed was to whisper his name before he leaned down and captured her lips with his.

A shower of ice sprayed over them from the other side of the gate. Kelsie jerked back as her son clomped off the ice looking every inch the rough and ready hockey player. His hair was disheveled, his jaw set at a pugnacious angle. The dark eyebrows he'd inherited from his mother slashed down over his brown eyes as he scowled at her and Alec as he walked past them, driving a hand into one of the many pockets of his camouflage pants to dig out two quarters for the soda machine.

"I'm sorry, Alec," Kelsie said, trying to keep her own temper in check. "Jeffrey's manners are nowhere near that bad most of the time. I don't know what's gotten into him."

"Really?"

"You think you do?"

He glanced at Kelsie. "I think he's not too crazy about having me interested in his mother. Is he close to his dad?"

Kelsie sighed as she watched her son drink his soda and crush the can. "He would like to be."

"What's that mean?" Alec asked gently.

"It means Jeff's father isn't terribly interested in his son at present. I'm sure that will change when Jeff is old enough to be on the varsity hockey team. Then he'll be valuable to Jack as something to brag about."

Feeling suddenly very tired, she leaned her head on Alec's shoulder without even thinking about it, and sighed. It felt good to have that solid square of muscle and bone to lean against, to have a strong arm cross her back and a firm hand cup her shoulder. When had she become so comfortable in Alec's presence? She didn't know, but when he asked her what had gone wrong with her marriage, she didn't hesitate to tell him.

"Nothing that hasn't happened to millions of marriages," she said. "We got married too young and grew apart. Ten years later we wanted different things. I wanted a station wagon and a house in the country. Jack wanted a Corvette and a receptionist named Dawn. What happened to yours?"

"I wasn't useful anymore," he said, stroking her shoulder in a soothing rhythm. It felt good to have Kelsie lean against him, to have her let her guard down for once. It was almost as good as an admission of need, and he very much wanted Kelsie to need him. "Vena's modeling career had taken off. She wanted someone more important."

He sat her up and winked at her. "How about a few more turns around the ice? Think you can keep up with me?"

"Ha! I think my grandma could keep up with you! Come on, let's see how many feet you can go before you land on your keister."

As she helped Alec struggle around the rink, Kelsie gave a lot of thought to the feelings he evoked in her. She hadn't had this kind of fun in so long—hell, she thought to herself, she'd never had this kind of fun. She genuinely liked being with Alec, and every time she saw him, her heart did a flip that could have gotten it a spot on the U.S. gymnastics team.

"Time! Time out!" Alec tripped his way to the boards. "I've got a cramp in my foot!"

"Giving up, McKnight?" Kelsie asked, turning and skating back to him.

He wagged a finger at her. "Next time we do something I'm good at. How are you on the ski slopes, Dorothy Hamill?"

Kelsie laughed. "Have you ever seen 'the agony of defeat' at the beginning of *Wide World of Sports*?"

Alec laughed, then a look of wonder came into his eyes. Hoping he wouldn't lose his balance and dump them both, he pulled Kelsie into his arms and brushed her hair back from her face. "Hey," he said, "you didn't try to tell me there wouldn't be a next time. Was that an oversight on your part, or are you coming around to my way of thinking?"

"I don't know," she said, taking a deep, ragged breath, her gaze locking on his as if to draw strength from the intense power there. "I still don't know if it can work, Alec. You've seen the kind of life I live."

"It's just a matter of making time for what's important, Kelsie," he said softly, his heart pounding above hers as he held her to him. "I have a busy life, too, but it's important to me to be able to see you." More important than he'd realized, he thought as he waited for her answer to his question. "Is it important to you to be able to see me?"

To see Alec was fast becoming as important to her as eating. Lately she found herself craving the sight of him more than she craved chocolate. Another wave of fear broke over her, but she shook it off.

"Yes," she said softly, but with the conviction of a shout.

His kiss was exuberant, jubilant, and ended with both of them crashing to the ice.

SIX

"No, Millard," Kelsie said, holding the phone between her shoulder and one ear as she tried to put an earring in her other earlobe. "I really don't think you should count on getting another crack at the Van Bryant deal."

"Has the decision been made, then?"

"No. They have to wait until Mr. Van Bryant gets back from Europe. I'm not holding out much hope though."

As Millard Krispin whined about how unfair Alec McKnight was being to Darwin, Jeffrey burst into the house, his face literally glowing with excitement. He'd been talking of nothing but the outing with his father to the college basketball game for a week. Now that the event was at hand, he seemed ready to explode with impatience.

Knowing Millard had another five minutes of droning left, Kelsie put a hand over the mouthpiece of the receiver. "Supper's ready; it's in the oven."

"I can't have supper, Mom; I won't have any room left for all the great junk at the ball game!"

"Silly me," she murmured as he charged off to his room. "Why should you have something nutritious when you can have chili dogs and caramel corn?"

"...And Darwin was upset for several days after that meeting," Millard finished.

Kelsie mouthed along with that part of his speech. He'd given it to her half a dozen times since the disaster in Alec's office. Alec. He had stopped by the shoot today and asked her to go to a hockey game with him tonight...and, lo and behold, she could since Jeffrey would be with his father and Elizabeth was going to a slumber party.

When she got off the phone she stuck the uneaten casserole into the refrigerator, pulled Randolph, the new kitty, out as she shut the door, then headed for the bathroom to finish her makeup. She had twenty minutes to get gorgeous before Alec arrived.

As she passed through the living room, the phone rang again. She snatched it up with a friendly hello that died on her lips when she heard Jack Connors's voice. With every word he spoke, she felt sicker and sicker. He was backing out on his promise to Jeffrey, and he wasn't even man enough to tell their son himself.

Jeffrey was sprawled on his bed, poring over a sports magazine, when Kelsie stepped into his room. The tan walls were papered with posters of his favorite sports stars and pictures of animals.

"This guy is so awesome!" Jeff raved, pointing to a picture of one of the Gopher basketball stars. "I'll bet he's gonna score about fifty points tonight."

Kelsie bit her lip as she sank down onto the

bed. She didn't think she'd ever dreaded anything so much in her life as having to tell her son he wasn't going to this ball game.

"Jeff," she said softly, barely able to look at him, "that was your dad on the phone."

As he sat up, the boy's expression went carefully blank, but he couldn't erase the look of fear from his warm brown eyes. He knew what was coming; Kelsie could see it. Jack had disappointed him too many times for him not to know. It didn't make it any easier for her to tell him.

"He can't make it tonight. Something came up. I'm so sorry, honey."

The day had come for him to find out there wasn't a Santa Claus, Kelsie thought as she watched his fragile hopes for a relationship with his father shatter into a million irreparable shards. Her eyes filled with tears as quickly as Jeffrey's did.

Fighting valiantly to not cry, Jeff looked down at his magazine. "Why does he hate me so much?"

He sounded so small and lost, it tore Kelsie's

heart in two and defeated her in her own battle against tears. They spilled over their boundaries and ran down her cheeks as she took her son in her arms and held him close.

"I'm sorry he's not the father you want him to be, Jeff," she whispered into his hair.

He let go of his pride, all the hurt and disappointment pouring out of him in heart-wrenching sobs. Kelsie wanted to do something, to say something to comfort him, but all she could do was hold him and whisper over and over how sorry she was, as if it were her fault because she had married Jack.

Alec turned his car into Kelsie's drive and parked it, whistling as he climbed out. He was going to have Kelsie all to himself for the entire evening. If luck was with him, Jeffrey would be spending the night with his father. Alec looked up at the cloudy black sky and whispered, *"Please."*

His overactive imagination had spent the better part of the afternoon mapping out the scenario. After the North Stars won the hockey game in a thrilling overtime finish, he would drive Kelsie back to her house—because it was closer to the Met Center—and spend the next five or six hours making love to her. If he could stand it, he would spend at least an hour undressing her, lingering over her lacy lingerie. His body tightened at the thought. Maybe he would have to make love to her first and then spend an hour peeling off her underwear, he thought, grinning as he punched the doorbell.

His grin faded as the door swung open to reveal Kelsie's tear-stained face.

"Kelsie! Honey, what's wrong?" He didn't wait to be asked in. He was through the door and had it closed behind him before Kelsie could sniffle. His cold hands stroked her mussed hair back from her face as he took in every nuance of her expression—the pale strain, the trembling of her soft mouth, the agony in her red-rimmed eyes. "What is it, sweetheart? Are the kids okay?"

Kelsie pulled together what little strength she had left; she felt so tired, so drained. "I'm sorry, Alec," she said in a rusty voice. "I can't go with you tonight. Jeff's dad backed out on taking him to the ball game."

It took a moment for the importance of what she'd said to sink in. Why would she be crying because of that? They could simply hire a sitter, couldn't they? Then the sound of crying came to him from somewhere in the house and he realized there was more to the situation than a minor disappointment and inconvenience.

He remembered what Kelsie had told him when he'd asked if Jeffrey was close to his father. "He would like to be," she had said. Now the little boy was sobbing his heart out because the one man who should have adored him hadn't seen fit to keep what was to Jeffrey a very important promise.

"I knew this was coming," Kelsie said, turning away from him. She raked a hand through her tangled blond hair and leaned against the back of the brown tweed recliner, her foot absently shoving stray shoes beneath it. She'd never felt more miserable or more of a failure. "I knew it was coming, but now that it's here, I don't know what to say to him. How do you tell a little boy his father doesn't care about anyone but himself?"

She swiped a rumpled tissue under her red-tipped nose and pounded her fist against the chair. "Dammit, I feel so helpless!"

Like magic Alec's arms were around her and her cheek was pressed to his chest, her tears soaking into his jewel-blue sweater. She leaned against him, her hands clutching at his back, because she couldn't muster the strength to pull away. She felt utterly helpless and it terrified her, just as it had terrified a shy farm girl with no job skills when she had first realized she would have to go it alone with two small children to raise. How she hated that feeling. How she had fought to overcome the need to be dependent on someone. Yet here she was, leaning on Alec.

Deep inside it felt right to have him hold her, her knight in shining armor. It frightened her, too, but instead of trying to deal with all the conflicting emotions within her, Kelsie did her best to push them to a far corner of her mind. She had more important things to worry about at the moment.

"I'm sorry about the hockey game, Alec. You can still go—"

"Would you mind if I have a little talk with Jeff?"

"You?" Kelsie asked skeptically as she pulled back enough to look up at him.

Alex tried to smile. "I know he hasn't exactly welcomed me with open arms, but I'd like to give it a shot."

He almost chickened out when he reached the door of Jeffrey's room. What did he know about kids? You used to be one, didn't you, he asked himself. His own father had taken him to more ball games and hockey games than he could remember. All he had to do was imagine how he would have felt if his dad had backed out on one of those special outings and brushed him off without a second thought.

Jeffrey was facedown on the bed, hiccuping and sniffling. Alec took a deep breath to steady his nerves, then sat down beside the boy.

"Tough break about that basketball game," he said, tugging methodically on his earlobe.

Jeffrey peered up at him with one bleary brown eye. "What's it to you?"

Alec shrugged. "I was just thinking. When I was about your age, my dad promised he'd take me with him to Lake Mille Lac for the opening of the fishing season. I don't think I talked about anything else for a month beforehand. I would have felt awful if he hadn't kept that promise."

Kelsie's son pressed his head back down on his forearm. "My dad hates me."

He sounded so forlorn, it nearly broke Alec's heart. It was hard to remember he was the same little ruffian that had regarded him with such disdain. Now Jeffrey was a little boy who'd had his dreams shattered, who felt deserted and unwanted by the most important man in his life. Alec wondered if Jack Connors had any idea what he'd done.

"Maybe he just doesn't know what's important, Jeff." It was difficult for Alex to imagine that the man even had a brain. The guy had let Kelsie and two beautiful children go. He was probably more deserving of pity than anything else.

He gave his head a shake and cleared his throat, glancing around the room at the posters of sports celebrities, several hockey players among them. Here goes my dream date, he thought to himself, not nearly as disappointed as he might have been.

"I know you're a big hockey fan," he said to Jeff. "I happened to get my hands on tickets to the Stars-Bruins game tonight. Your mom said she'd go with me, but I don't think she really wants to. Besides, it'd be more fun with another guy along.... You interested?"

Jeffrey raised his head and turned to give Alec a long, suspicious look.

"I'd really like it if you went with me," Alec said, surprised at how much he meant it.

"You mean it?" Jeff asked hesitantly.

Alex gave the boy his most sincere look. "I wouldn't say it if I didn't mean it, Jeff."

The boy dodged the man's gaze as he sat up and swung his legs over the side of the bed. "I haven't been very nice to you."

"I don't have anything against starting over," Alec said, offering his hand. There was only a second's hesitation before it was met by a smaller, chubbier one.

"Go get washed up," Alec said with a wink and a grin. "We can still make the opening face-off."

Jeffrey dashed for the door, pausing when he reached it and turning back toward Alec. "Did you catch anything on that fishing trip?"

Alec's grin widened in remembrance. "A couple of bullheads and a major league case of poison ivy. It was the best time I ever had."

Kelsie woke up on the couch at eleven o'clock with the television rumbling in the corner and the lamp turned on low on the end table. She felt as if she'd been sleeping for years. The three cats sat in a row on the floor, staring up at her. They weren't allowed on the good furniture.

Trying to shake the cobwebs from her head, Kelsie sat up, rubbing her eyes. She shooed the cats away. "You know I hate it when you guys stare at me," she complained. "It gives me the creeps."

The cats trotted away with their tails in the air.

The hockey game would be over by now, she thought. Alec and Jeff should be on their way home. She wondered how the evening had gone. Alec had no experience with kids, and Jeffrey could be a pistol. They had probably killed each other. She'd been shocked that her son had agreed to go with Alec. She'd been shocked that Alec had offered to take the boy.

That's the kind of thing knights do, Kelsie, she told herself, rubbing her hands up and down her arms to get her circulation going. A girl could get used to being rescued by him. But it wouldn't be a good idea, a weak voice cautioned her from somewhere in the back of her mind.

She sighed and tried to comb her fingers through her hair. She was too tired to listen to dire warnings from her psyche. Not tonight, she told the little voice, hoping she could dredge up the energy to make a pot of coffee.

The sound of a car turning into her driveway gave her the incentive to get off the couch and walk to the front door. She swung the door back, her eyes widening at the sight of Alec carrying a sleeping Jeffrey toward her.

In that instant Kelsie fell deeply, irrevocably in love with him. Or perhaps it just suddenly hit her that she'd been in love with him for some time and simply hadn't recognized the feeling for what it was. Either way, the realization left her feeling exhilarated and frightened all at once, like the gravity-defying rides at the state fair had.

Never uttering a word, she followed Alec to Jeffrey's room and watched as he eased her son down onto his bed, slipped off the boy's sneakers, and covered him with a quilt. Only after they had retreated to the hall did either one speak.

"I never saw anyone sleep so soundly," Alec whispered. "He was out before we got to the parking lot exit and never moved a muscle the whole way home."

Kelsie smiled. "He's like that. He'll be out now until breakfast tomorrow. You'd never believe he had insomnia as a baby. Thanks for taking him, Alec. It really meant a lot to Jeffrey." And to me, she added silently.

"What are knights for?" He shrugged. "Taking little boys to hockey games is on the list a few notches below carrying damsels across crocodile-infested moats."

"So who won?" she asked, leaning into Alec as he slipped his arm around her waist.

"Boston. Five to four in overtime."

"Too bad."

He shook his head. The evening wasn't going exactly the way he'd dreamed, but he couldn't honestly say he felt like complaining. He had genuinely enjoyed taking Kelsie's son to the game. He had to laugh at himself—the confirmed bachelor playing father and liking it. "We had a great time."

Kelsie stopped and smiled up at him. "Did you really?"

"We did," he assured her, his dimples creasing his cheeks as he looked down at her. With a little imagination and a few props, she might have looked like a bag lady. Her hair was a mess, her makeup long gone. She wore a pair of light gray sweat pants and a baggy red top that buttoned down the front and looked like half of a matched set of thermal underwear. Wool socks bagged around her ankles. Alec thought she looked like an angel. "Did we wake you?"

She shook her head. "I was about to make some coffee. Want some?"

"No," he answered, steering her toward the couch. "I want you."

Kelsie's eyes widened, but she said nothing. They had been headed toward this for a long time, she thought, perhaps from the day they'd met. For it to happen tonight, when she'd discovered she was in love with him, seemed right.

Alec sat them both down and took Kelsie into his arms for a long series of deep, drugging kisses. His mouth took complete yet gentle command of hers. Her surrender was unconditional. She sighed as his tongue slid over hers, and she drank in the warm taste of him. Her hands came up to cradle his face, her fingers gliding back into the dark silk of his hair and down to the strong muscles of the back of his neck. It seemed as though they kissed for hours, never rushing as they sampled the tastes and textures of each other's mouth as they adjusted angles and degrees of pressure.

When Alec finally eased her away from him, he looked into her eyes and very deliberately raised his hands to the top button of her jersey. He had to see her, touch her, taste her. Kelsie made no move to stop him. She sat patiently with her hands in lap, her soft blue eyes on his as his fingers freed one button then another. Finally he pushed the garment open, his breath catching in his throat as he bared her breasts.

They were lovely, small but full and proud, with dusky brown nipples that had hardened and jutted forward, begging for his touch. Mesmerized, he stroked his fingertips down the sides of the soft globes, thinking he could feel them swell and tighten with desire as his own body swelled and tightened. His thumbs caressed the center buds, hardly touching them at first, increasing the pressure until he was rubbing them over and over.

Kelsie's head fell back as she gasped for air. It had been so long since she had been touched by a man, and then, never like this, with such exquisite care and attention and patience. She loved Alec. Giving herself to him was her way of wholly accepting that knowledge. She wanted to give him pleasure but had never dreamed of being given so much pleasure in return. When he leaned forward and touched her breast with his lips, she thought she would go mad. When he took the tip of her breast into his mouth and began to suck, she was certain she had.

His tongue stroked the aching peak, his teeth grazed across it, his lips massaged it. Kelsie drove her fingers through his hair and cradled him there at her breast, never wanting him to stop. She lay back, arching into the delicious heat of his mouth, gasping when his hand closed over her aching femininity and he began to explore her through her clothing.

His fingers touched and teased until she could no longer stand the barrier of garments between her and his caresses. Desperate for more intimate contact, she reached down and plucked at the drawstring waist of her sweat pants, lifting her hips for Alec to pull them down.

"So pretty," he whispered, pressing kisses

along the fine line of downy blond hair that trailed over her tummy. His fingers slid into the nest of dark tawny curls between her thighs, wringing a soft moan from her as he parted the petals of feminine flesh and began his exploring anew.

Alec was amazed at his own patience. His body had been ready to take hers half an hour ago, and she was certainly ready for him, yet he was content to lay there, touching and teasing her and watching her sanity slip away. She would be wild in his arms, he thought, gritting his teeth at the surge in his loins as he imagined what their joining would feel like. Heaven—that was what he wanted to give her.

She chanted his name in a whisper-soft litany as his thumb found her most sensitive flesh and began stroking while he eased two fingers deep inside her.

"Alec!" she sobbed, writhing against his hand. "Alec, please!"

He stretched out on top of her, letting her feel his hardness through his jeans. He pressed against her, rocked against her as he kissed her deeply. "Are you on the pill, honey?"

"Yes," she whispered, glad she had renewed her prescription as her hands clutched at the sweater he wore, trying to drag it up his back.

"Maybe we should go to your bedroom," he suggested, nipping on her earlobe.

"No," she said, trembling hands reaching for him. He growled low in his throat as her fingers slid inside his pants and she touched him for the first time. He was solid and hot and as ready for her as she was for him. "Now, Alec, please."

How many times had he dreamed of hearing her say those words? Now he wasn't only hearing them, he was going to live out the rest of his dream of making love to Kelsie. He reached down to shove his jeans out of their way, but his hands stilled on his waistband as a plaintive voice called out from several rooms away.

"Mom? Mom, I think I'm gonna be sick."

All the passion suddenly went out of their groans. Kelsie pushed her hair out of her eyes and hastily began to rearrange her clothes. Alec sat up, half laughing half crying, cradling his head in his hands. Every inch of his body ached with frustrated desire. He felt like he'd been flogged from head to foot with a rubber hose.

"This is what I get for letting him have that last chili dog," he muttered.

SEVEN

"OUCH! DAMN!" KELSIE snapped as she stuck herself in the eye with her mascara wand. Tears dragged a stream of black down her cheek.

"Damn!" the parrot mimicked.

With one eye Kelsie peered at her son in the doorway of the bathroom. "Jeffrey, get that bird off your head."

"But you said I could take him out of the cage."

"I didn't say you could wear him for a hat," she said, dabbing at her stinging eye with a wet washcloth, dripping water onto her white silk robe.

The brilliant blue bird squawked and began chanting, "Love me, baby. Love me, baby. Love me, baby."

"Pirate," Kelsie said in a threatening tone. Hyacinth macaws weren't great talkers to begin with, but this one's vocabulary made Kelsie wish it were completely mute. The Humane Society had rescued him from a Mississippi River barge. What words and phrases the bird knew had been learned from sailors on a garbage scow.

Jeffrey and his pet made a hasty retreat. Kelsie returned to the mirror to start over on her makeup, calling out to her daughter, "Elizabeth! Did you find that black purse for me?"

Elizabeth appeared in the doorway and leaned against the jamb. "Yes, Mom. That's the third time you've asked me."

"Sorry." Kelsie stared in the mirror, trying to decide if she had messed up her lipstick again or if her mouth was really that oddly shaped. Her stomach was dancing a jig.

"Why are you so nervous about this date?

You've been seeing Mr. McKnight for a long time."

Kelsie watched the blush creep into her pale cheeks. Why was she nervous? Because she and Alec had very nearly made love on the couch last night, and tonight smart money would bet he was going to make certain they didn't have any interruptions, and now that she'd had a whole day to think about it, she was getting cold feet.

Elizabeth was watching her with amused blue eyes, calmly waiting for an answer.

"Because. Alec said he's taking me somewhere very special for dinner and dancing, and I want everything to be perfect, that's why."

"Where's he taking you?"

"It's a surprise."

"He's *sooo* cute, Mom. Do you think he's getting serious? Maybe he's going to pop the question tonight! Maybe that's why he's taking you someplace special. Are you going to say yes?"

Kelsie leveled a stern look at her daughter. "I think you're getting way ahead of the game. Alec and I have known each other only a few weeks, honey. We're having a nice time together, but I wouldn't start looking for a bridesmaid dress if I were you. I couldn't honestly say either Alec or I are ready to get married again, and I don't want you asking him about it either."

"Mom! What do you take me for, some kind of geek?" Elizabeth asked, looking highly offended—a look that almost instantly transformed itself to one of excited conspiracy. "You'd say yes, wouldn't you? He's *sooo* cute!"

A scowl from Kelsie sent Elizabeth away giggling. Giving up on her makeup, she padded barefoot to her room to dress. One of the great advantages of selling Naughty Nighties lingerie was the huge discount she got on merchandise. Over the last few years Kelsie had not been able to splurge on anything other than necessities, but, because of her discount, she had accumulated a lot of nice underwear. When she hadn't been able to treat herself in any other way, she had been able to go to her dresser and pull out something wonderfully silky and lacy and sexy to wear.

She surveyed what she'd laid out on the bed for

this very special night, wondering what Alec would think when he saw it. Dropping her robe on a chair, she slipped into the brief black lace panties. The matching garter belt came next, followed by the sheer black stockings with the seam up the back. Finally she wiggled a snug, lacy black camisole on over her head, tugged it down into place, and took a look at herself in the mirror above her dresser.

She looked as if she had a hell of a lot more experience than she did. Quelling the urge to tear the garments off and replace them with more ordinary versions, she turned away from the mirror, hoping Alec wouldn't end up accusing her of false advertising.

She stepped into a black lace petticoat and fastened it, then she put her black velvet dress on and turned back to the mirror. It was her one really fancy dress, which she'd picked up at an after-Christmas sale the year before. The lines were simple: a snug bodice with a simple round neckline that revealed nothing, a gently gathered skirt that stood out a bit with its petticoat beneath. The one sexy feature of the dress was the back. The upper part was cut out and crisscrossed with two straps studded with rhinestones. The look was demure yet alluring. The rich black velvet invited one's touch and turned Kelsie's fair complexion to pearly cream.

She was just finishing tying a ribbon of black lace into her hair when she heard the doorbell ring.

"Hi, Alec." Jeffrey greeted his new friend at the door with a high five.

Alec grinned. "Hi, sport. Nice hood ornament you've got there."

"Jeffrey, I told you to get that bird off your head!" Kelsie yelled, hobbling into the room with one shoe on and one in her hand.

Pirate shrieked and stretched his wings out. "Hot mama, hot mama, hot mama!"

"I'll have to agree with him there," Alec said smoothly, his laser-blue gaze burning down from the top of her head to the tip of her one bare big toe.

Kelsie turned scarlet. That patented skin-searing look of his combined with his cat-that-got-the-canary smile was almost enough to send her running for cover. Her body's response to him was so strong, so swift—and he was half a room away! What was going to happen when he got his hands on her?

Her massive attack of nerves automatically flipped her switch for inane prattle. She forced her eyes to focus on the parrot, still perched atop her son's head as he reached up to feed it a palm nut. "Like most hyacinth macaws, he has a very limited vocabulary. We got him from the Humane Society. He had a severe vitamin deficiency and had lost a lot of his plumage due to—"

Alec held up a hand to cut her off. "I think I caught the special on PBS," he said, amused at her obvious nervousness. He winked at Kelsie's daughter. "Hi, Elizabeth."

The girl's blush rivaled her mother's. She glanced down and murmured a hello.

"Now, we'll be kind of late, honey," Kelsie said to her daughter, jamming her foot into her other shoe. "But I'll call and check on you—"

"Mom!" Elizabeth groaned.

"Jeffrey, put the bird away and behave yourself."

"There's a buck in it for you," Alec whispered to the boy as Kelsie slipped her coat on.

Jeffrey's eyes lit up. "All right!"

Once they were in Alec's car and on the road, Kelsie began fidgeting in her seat. "Where are we going?"

Alec smiled enigmatically. "It's a surprise."

"I hope I'm dressed right. Do I look all right?"

"*Gorgeous* is the word I'd use," he said, sending her a slow, bone-melting smile as they waited for a traffic light to change. "Beautiful."

The word caressed her like a silken hand. Kelsie shivered in spite of her heavy wool coat. Remembrance of last night glowed in his eyes and started a steady burn in the pit of her stomach. To distract herself she said, "It's not too much?"

"No."

"Too little?"

"Honey, I promise you, you are dressed perfectly for where we're going."

"Good."

She looked him over as he piloted the car north. GQ would have loved him; he wore clothes with such ease. They draped over his body the same way Kelsie wanted to—gracefully, lovingly. He wore a trendy casual suit of black tweed flecked prominently with the same riveting blue of his eyes. His shirt was the same color—the color of seduction, Kelsie thought to herself. People thought red was sexy. They obviously had never encountered Alec McKnight's eyes. There couldn't be anything more sexy than the way his eyes had looked as he'd gazed down at her the moment before they'd been so rudely interrupted last night.

There won't be any interruptions tonight, she thought. A wave of heat engulfed her. Her nipples tightened on her suddenly heavy breasts. She crossed her legs to try to ease the dull ache that had begun between her thighs. She turned up the radio and forced herself to memorize the words to every song she heard in an attempt to get her mind off sex.

Alec did nothing to help the situation. He remained unusually silent, tuned in to Kelsie's sexual tension, content to let it build until the air in the car hummed with it.

Finally he turned the BMW off the street. A paved wooded drive led them to a fancy triplex cedar-sided town house.

"Where are we?" Kelsie asked cautiously.

"My place," he said, helping her out of the car.

Her pulse jumped erratically. "Forget something?"

"Not a thing."

"I thought we were going to dinner."

"We are," he said, leading her up the walk. He opened the door, bowing to her as he motioned her inside. "Welcome to Chez Alexander, where the dance floor is never crowded and the service is *very* personal."

Kelsie stepped into the foyer, then followed Alec up the steps to the upper level of his home. Soft lights reflected off the highly polished oak floor in the kitchen and formal dining area. Beyond, a thick off-white carpet stretched across the living room to a wall of glass. The deck on the other side overlooked part of Lake Minnetonka. The furniture looked comfortable and expensive, but what really impressed Kelsie was that the place was immaculate. There wasn't so much as a throw pillow out of place.

Alec hung her coat in the closet, then went to turn on the music. Notes from a soft, bluesy sax drifted on the air from the stereo speakers as he lit a fire in the brick fireplace. Kelsie was looking over the table set for two when he came and pulled a chair out for her.

"Did you do all this?" she asked. A navy blue homespun tablecloth stretched under two settings of gleaming white china but no flatware. He lighted a trio of tall white tapers in silver candlesticks. A small silver bowl was overflowing with white carnations.

"Mmm-hmm," he murmured, his teeth nipping at her pearl earrings as he bent over her from behind. "For you. For us."

A shallow, shuddering breath failed to fill Kelsie's lungs. She forced herself to glance to the open kitchen with its oak cupboards and tiled counters. "Are you a good cook?"

"I have my specialties"—his voice brushed over her as his fingertips trailed down her throat—"in the kitchen ... and out."

"Oh." The word was little more than an exhalation of breath, a puff of air that didn't disturb the flames at the tops of the candles.

Flames. Oh, dear. Kelsie groaned inwardly. You're way out of your league here, kid, she told herself. Everything Alec said and did seemed purposefully seductive. He was trying to arouse her to a flash point of desire and was succeeding famously. Her skin was alive to every sensation, her breasts felt as if they were straining the bodice of her dress, and he hadn't even served the appetizer yet. She was going to be frantic by the end of the meal. She crossed her legs and tried to think of unsexy things like iguanas and spotted hyenas.

Alec poured champagne into crystal fluted glasses, then seated himself across the small table from Kelsie so he could make full use of his most lethal weapons—hypnotic eyes bluer than all the lakes in Minnesota put together, and a smile that could charm the starch out of the stiffest matron. Giving her a dose of both, he removed the cover from the silver try he'd brought to the table, revealing a dozen huge strawberries dipped in chocolate.

Kelsie groaned aloud. "You are a dirty player, Alec."

Alec grinned roguishly. "I warned you I would take full advantage of any weakness. *Bon appétit*, sweetheart."

Eating with the fingers—something that was not at all uncommon at her house—seemed suddenly very naughty here... naughty and fun. They watched each other nibble at the delicacies, trading smiles and giggles.

Alec took the tray back to the kitchen. Stripping off his suit jacket, he began rolling up the sleeves of his blue shirt. "Now for my world-famous house specialty." He dug an anonymous-looking brown paper carton out of his freezer. "Alexander L. McKnight's Knock 'Em Dead Hot Fudge Sundae."

"For the main course?" Kelsie giggled, draining her champagne glass for the second time.

"Why not?"

"What's for dessert?"

"Chocolate soufflé."

"Oh, Alec," she said, "you're so wicked."

He chuckled devilishly. "You bet."

Kelsie sat at the table while he prepared the sundaes, allowing him to wait on her. That in itself was a wonderful treat. Kelsie usually spent her meals bobbing up and down out of her chair like a human yo-yo, waiting on her children. When at last he placed the bowl before her and handed her a sterling spoon, she sampled the dish as if she were a queen taste-testing the royal caviar.

It was sheer heaven. Vanilla and chocolate ice cream drenched in rich, thick fudge that had been heated to a temperature that wouldn't immediately melt the frozen treat, topped with real whipped cream and crowned with a bright red cherry.

"What do you think? As if I need to ask," Alec said, grinning smugly at the look of rapture on Kelsie's face.

"Words can't begin to describe it. The ice cream alone would be wonderful. What kind is it?"

He shook his head. "I'm not giving my secrets away. I will tell you it's made fresh up north by Norwegian bachelor farmers and sold locally in only one teeny tiny little gourmet shop that you have to have a password to get into."

When their "dinner" was over, Alec led her to the living room, poured one snifter of brandy for the two of them, and opened a box of imported chocolates. Kelsie kicked her shoes off and accepted Alec's silent invitation to curl up next to him on the sofa. The champagne she'd consumed had taken the edge off her nervousness, but it was the chocolate that was making her feel tipsy. She couldn't remember the last time she'd given free rein to her undying craving for chocolate.

She snuggled against Alec's side, his arm around her shoulders, her legs tucked up on the sofa, the full skirt of her velvet dress spreading out around her. He fed her bites of the bittersweet candy, then let her sip from the brandy glass at the same spot he'd used. All the while, music swirled around them. It seemed perfectly natural when Alec tipped her chin up and kissed her, his lips warm and pliant against hers.

The kiss lingered, turned into another kiss,

then another—all of them slow and hot. He tasted of brandy and chocolate and desire, and Kelsie couldn't decide which was the most intoxicating. She wasn't sure she cared, she thought as she shifted positions and went on kissing him, her hands framing his face, her fingers running into his hair. Alec's hands went to the snug waist of Kelsie's dress, holding her steady and enjoying the feel of velvet beneath his fingers.

"Let's dance," he whispered against her swelling lips.

He pulled her up from the sofa into his arms, pressing her body to his and marveling at the way she fit. He wrapped his arms around her and let his head drop down so his breath teased the tendrils of baby-blond hair near her ear.

"Isn't this better than a crowded dance floor?" he asked, tightening his arms around her.

"Mmm-hmmm," she answered, her eyes drifting shut as she pressed her cheek into the hollow of his shoulder.

"Nobody bumping into us, no one stepping on our toes, no interruptions—"

Kelsie's head shot up. "I have to call home!"

Better now than later, Alec told himself as he gritted his teeth and nodded. He led her to the phone that sat beside the couch on an antique cherry table. He stood directly behind her as she dialed, refusing to stop touching her. His hands stroked down her sides in a featherlike caress as his lips nibbled at the nape of her neck.

"Elizabeth? Hi, honey, is everything going okay?" Kelsie asked, trying unsuccessfully to ignore Alec's sensual ministrations.

"Fine, Mom. We're just watching TV."

"Did you make your cookies?" she asked breathlessly as Alec's hand swept down over the curve of her hip.

"Yeah. Are you having fun? Where are you?"

Kelsie bit back a groan as Alec cupped her breast, his thumb teasing her nipple. "Ohhh, yes, we're having...fun."

"Are you okay? You sound strange."

"I'm...just...a little out of breath," she answered. Alec went on massaging her breast while his other hand stroked down over her belly and lower, pressing her back into his arousal. His

tongue traced the shell of her ear. "We've...
been...dancing."

By the time she hung up the phone, Kelsie was
ready to collapse. Select parts of her body had
grown so heavy with desire, it seemed her legs
could no longer support her. Alec turned her in his
arms, molding her to him for another long, drugging kiss, bending her back over his arm and trailing his hot lips down the graceful column of her
throat.

"I think it's time to move this party to more
cozy quarters," he murmured. He led her down
the hall to his bedroom, holding her firmly to his
side as if he knew her knees weren't steady
enough to carry her.

Even though she was nervous, Kelsie took in
the details of Alec's room. It was spacious and as
neat as the rest of the house. The walls were a
soft shade of blue, the floor polished oak warmed
by a deep blue Oriental carpet where the four-
poster stood. The same fireplace that warmed the
living room crackled in this room, too, faced on
this side of the wall with the same weathered
brick and a thick oak mantel. Also as in the living

room, one wall was made completely of glass and opened onto the cedar deck that overlooked the lake.

A small brass lamp burned softly beside the bed, creating an inviting oasis of warm light. Taking Kelsie's hand, Alec led her toward it, noticing immediately the slight hesitation in her step. He turned toward her with a questioning look, which was met by one full of uncertainty.

"What's the matter, honey?" he asked gently. "Don't tell me you're going shy on me after last night."

Kelsie bit her lip, her gaze darting around the room. "Last night was so...spontaneous. Now I've had a whole day to get nervous and..." Finally she met his gaze. "It's been a long time for me, Alec."

He gave her a sweet smile, running the back of his hand down her cheek. "You don't forget about making love, sweetheart. It's like riding a bike, only it feels a hell of a lot better."

The comment earned him a nervous giggle as Kelsie stepped into his arms. "And if I fall off, I climb right back on, right?"

"That's horseback riding." He laughed.

"Oh. Right."

"Of course," he said, letting his imagination run away with him, "it could apply here. We'll see." He kissed her hair and rubbed her back to relax her as they stood beside his bed. "Don't worry, honey. We'll talk each other through it. A little coaching doesn't hurt, and I don't want you to be afraid to tell me what you like or don't like. There shouldn't be any secrets between us in here, no barriers."

Kelsie couldn't stop a little shiver from passing through her. She and Jack had never talked during sex. Making love with Alec was going to be very different. Very special, she amended, relying heavily on the power of positive thinking. As she had learned to do in every other aspect of her life, she got a firm handle on her fears and forced them out of her mind. She could be the kind of lover Alec needed if she let her love for him guide her.

She looked up at him with a tiny smile, hoping her voice wouldn't sound too unsteady. "I'd like to undress you."

"I'd like that too." He pressed a soft kiss to her lips, then led her hands to the knot in his tie. At first she fumbled a bit with the strip of black and blue silk, but Alec murmured words of encouragement, making her giggle and stealing her jitters away. When the tie hung loose, she boldly moved to the buttons of his shirt. She expected him to stop her somewhere along the way, but he made no move to do so, and after a few moments he stood magnificently naked before her.

Feeling more daring, Kelsie stood back and let her gaze devour him. He was beautifully made, lean and elegant and in better shape than she would have expected a desk jockey to be. The muscles of his chest weren't bulky but were clearly delineated. His stomach was taut. His manhood stood out prominently from a nest of ebony curls. He was beautiful, and he would be hers, hers to love and please. The thought sent tremors of excitement through Kelsie.

At the sudden darkening of her eyes, Alec growled low in his throat and reached for her.

"My turn," he said, feeling every bit as possessive as he sounded.

The black velvet dress and petticoat were quickly dispatched to a chair. When he got a look at what she was wearing underneath, Alec's eyes turned midnight-blue with desire. He felt as if he'd had the wind knocked out of him. The words he whispered beneath his breath would have been considered swear words if they hadn't been uttered so reverently.

"You wore this for me, didn't you, sweetheart?" he asked. He was touched because he knew how nervous she was, and yet she'd worked up the courage to wear erotic lingerie for him.

Kelsie nodded, her eyes wide with uncertainty. "Do you like it?"

His answer was a deep, tortured, masculine groan.

Alec drew her to him, then turned her so she could see their reflection in the large mirror above his dresser. "You can't know how many times I've pictured you just like this," he said, freeing her hair from its ribbon of lace. "With your hair down, wearing nothing but black lace. So pretty. So feminine. All mine."

He nipped at her shoulder, keeping his gaze on Kelsie's in the mirror. His hands came up to cup her breasts through the camisole, kneading them, testing their weight, teasing her nipples with his fingertips. With his teeth he dragged down one strap from her shoulder and his fingers peeled the garment away from one breast, exposing it to the soft amber light.

Kelsie felt faint. She'd never been a party to anything so arousing, so erotic. She could feel Alec's hands on her fevered skin, see them caressing her, see her own body reacting to him. Her eyelids drooped heavily over passion-darkened eyes, her skin was flushed, her lips swollen and red from his kisses, her breasts swelling in his hands. His thumb caressed the sensitive, distended peak, wringing a little gasp from her. She bit her lip and arched back against him.

"You like that, honey?" he said against her throat, satisfied with the nod she gave him.

Sliding his hands down over the gentle swell of

her tummy, he hooked his thumbs in the waistband of the scrap of lace she wore as panties and eased them down, revealing a delta of dark curls he longed to comb his fingers through. Kelsie moaned, her head lolling back against his shoulder as her knees gave out entirely.

Alec laid her gently on the bed, removing her stockings, garter belt, and panties with fingers that shook with anticipation. Unable to wait much longer, he stretched himself out above her, settling his body down along the soft length of hers. His mouth sought out her one exposed breast to kiss and suck, then dragged across her chest to the other to give it the same treatment through the gauzy barrier of sheer black lace.

Kelsie was sure she was losing her mind. Her control was gone. She writhed and arched beneath him like a wild thing. As Alec's hands and mouth drove her sanity to the edge, cries of pleasure rose in her throat that she tried unsuccessfully to stifle. She had never felt this way, so close to being totally uninhibited. It frightened her a little, and she tensed.

Alec knew what she was feeling. He was feeling it, too, and he was experienced enough to know it was a rare and wonderful thing. They were so in tune to each other and so hungry for each other that all barriers were slipping away. If Kelsie would relax, he was certain what was about to take place would transcend anything either of them had ever known.

"Don't fight it, sweetheart," he said in her ear as he slipped his hand between her thighs to find her hot and ready for him. "Just let go, sweet. Just let it happen."

He stroked her until she was sobbing for him, beyond holding back. Parting her thighs with his knees, he sought entry, almost losing what little control he had left when Kelsie's hand closed around his shaft to guide him into her.

"Oh, Alec, it feels so good!" she said with a moan, arching her hips up to his as he pressed deep with a slow, careful thrust.

"Oh, yes. *Sooo* good," he answered, forcing himself to be still for a moment while they savored their first union. Leaning on his elbows, he brushed her tangled hair back from her face and gazed down at her. "I dreamed of this. Of being inside you and having your legs wrapped around me, pulling me deeper and deeper."

"I dreamed it too," she whispered, gasping a little as her body adjusted to the size and strength of him. "Of having my arms around you and having you inside me so deep and so hard." She managed a weak laugh. "This is a lot more satisfying than a dream."

Alec lowered his head to kiss her, murmuring against her lips, "No dream ever came close to this."

From that moment words lost all importance. Kelsie and Alec moved together, sometimes slowly, sometimes with a wild urgency. They rolled across the bed, tangling in the sheets as they sought positions that allowed more closeness or different degrees of sensation. In the end, Kelsie straddled Alec, their gazes locked, and each watched the other's face as passion rewarded them with a pleasure that soared beyond the realm of mortal description.

For a long while afterward they lay together,

drifting on a sea of contentment, too exhausted to speak, too happy to move. Alec had managed to pull the down comforter over them, and they cuddled together, sighing and nuzzling and kissing while the fire popped and sizzled across the room.

At long last Kelsie raised her head from his shoulder and smiled down at him like a cat drunk on cream. "That was—"

He pressed a finger to her lips, his dimples cutting into his cheeks. "Let's not even try to put it into words."

"For you too?" she asked, a little nervous. She had been so lost in the pleasure he had given her, she hadn't had time to worry whether or not Alec was finding her lacking in any way.

"You better believe it," he said, rolling her beneath him. His hands cupping her buttocks, he lifted her hips and slid into her again, loving her gently this time.

Afterward, he climbed out of bed, stoked the fire, then left the room, returning with a full snifter of brandy and what was left of the box of chocolates. They sat up in bed sharing the drink, feeding each other bites of candy. After the third piece Alec insisted on licking the chocolate off Kelsie's fingers, then she reciprocated, and suddenly the food and drink were forgotten.

It was just after one when Kelsie finally looked at the clock. Alec had turned the light off and they lay entwined under the covers. Moonlight flooded the room through the wall of glass. The embers of the fire glowed in the grate. On the stand beside the bed the brilliant green digits of Alec's alarm clock proclaimed the party was over.

"Alec?" Kelsie whispered, not certain whether he was asleep or awake.

"What, honey?"

"I have to go home."

He said nothing for a moment, then his arms tightened around her and he uttered one word. "Stay."

"I can't. You know I can't. I wish I could," she said, feeling a strange sense of panic. She wished she could stay with him and yet, she wanted to be home. *Home* and *safe* were the words that came to mind. How ridiculous. She'd never felt safer than when she had Alec's arms around her. Then she remembered the first time he'd kissed her and how she hadn't felt safe until she'd gotten a door between them.

"I know you can't stay," he said. "I was being selfish. I'm sorry."

The drive back to Eden Prairie was silent and too short. Kelsie sat next to Alec with his arm around her and her head on his shoulder. She felt a need to be close to him after what they had shared, but in a way she couldn't understand, he seemed distant, as if for some reason he had retreated within himself. He seemed almost as cold and unapproachable as he had when she had first seen him in his office. She couldn't think of anything to say to break the spell.

When they reached her house, Alec walked her to the door.

"Can I see you tomorrow night?" he asked, shoving his hands into the pockets of his heavy black wool topcoat.

Kelsie frowned. "I volunteered to chaperone Elizabeth's Junior Achievers group to a craft fair in Stillwater, and they're having a party afterward."

"Monday?" he asked, his jaw tightening.

"Jeff has Cub Scouts. I'm sorry."

Alec reined back a sigh and tried again. "What about Tuesday?"

"I have lingerie parties Tuesday and Thursday nights, and Wednesday is the League of Businesswomen."

Shaking his head, Alec let go of the harsh sigh in a puff of cold white breath. He gave her a wry smile that held no humor and less charm. "Why don't you just call me when you think you can work me into your calendar."

His tone of voice stung, a pain that was reflected in the look she gave him. "Alec, that's not fair. You know I have responsibilities—"

"Well, forgive me if I think what we have together is a little more important than the League of Businesswomen. I love you, Kelsie. Fit *that* into your schedule," he said, and stormed back to his car, anger obvious in every stride.

Stunned, Kelsie watched him go, unable to move or speak. Finally she bolted off the steps and ran after him, but he had already climbed into the car. "Alec, wait!" she called as he shifted the BMW into drive. "Alec, I love you!"

Her voice trailed off into the still of the night, like the cloud of exhaust from the sleek black car as it headed back toward Minnetonka.

"Damn," she muttered, suddenly colder inside than the November night.

Alec lay fully clothed across his bed, unaware of what time it was, and uncaring. The night sky had turned as black as his mood and was sending down a shower of snow, snow as cold as the lump of fear in his belly.

When had he fallen in love with Kelsie Connors? Did it matter? He was in love with her now, in deeper than he'd ever been in his life. And he was scared. Vena had left his heart battered and bruised.

Now he needed Kelsie to need him. He needed to be important to her. These were feelings he'd kept hidden from himself; uncovering them was frightening. It was terrifying to suddenly discover he was vulnerable, that his knight's armor couldn't protect him—and it was ironic. In the beginning he had set out to rescue Kelsie. Now he was the one who needed rescuing, and it was entirely possible that Kelsie would think herself too busy to save him.

EIGHT

ALEC SAT AT his desk, staring blindly at the papers spread out across the smooth oak top. His secretary, Ms. Bond, rambled in with a cigarette dangling from her lip, a stack of mail in one meaty hand, and a stoneware mug of steaming coffee in the other.

"Can you believe that Art Parnell?" she complained in her Yosemite Sam voice. "He actually wants to hire cocktail waitresses in skimpy Santa outfits for the Christmas party. Sexist creep."

When no comment came from her boss, Ms.

Bond gave him a look, plunking down his coffee cup and mail. "Are you having an out-of-body experience or what?"

"Huh?" Alec's head snapped up. He hated it when Ms. Bond snuck up on him. A person needed a little preparation time before looking up into that Hulk Hogan face of hers.

"Maybe we should feed you this coffee intravenously."

"Coffee. Thanks," he said, sipping gingerly at the black brew. "What were you saying about Art Parnell?"

"He's a moron." Ms. Bond had no regard for the man's rank at Glendenning. She had been with the company since day one. No one was going to mess with *her* position.

Alec made a face. "Tell me something I don't know," he complained testily.

"All right, Eugene Van Bryant is back from Belgium with his child bride. He's coming to this office in an hour, and you're sitting here like something out of *Dawn of the Dead*."

A scowl pulled his straight dark brows low over his eyes. "I knew all that too," he said.

Unintimidated, Ms. Bond leaned across the desk and patted Alec's cheek like a worried mother. "This isn't like you. Pull yourself together. Consider my reputation. How would I face the other secretaries if word got out my boy-wonder boss was slipping?"

Alec forced a facsimile of his wily smile. Ms. Bond was the original battle ax, but he wouldn't have traded her for any three other secretaries in the place. She was efficient, undyingly loyal, and no one got past her desk without an appointment. "Don't worry, Ms. Bond, I'll charm his socks off."

When Ms. Bond had gone, Alec leaned back in his chair, heaving a sigh and rubbing his right earlobe between thumb and forefinger. His secretary was right, this wasn't like him. One of his most notable attributes had always been the ability to attack a project with awesomely single-minded determination. There hadn't been a distraction invented that could sway him from a job. Until Kelsie Connors.

Thoughts of Kelsie took precedence over everything because he was in love with her. He was in so deep, it scared him silly. He had even taken a day off work to try to get a handle on his feelings. He had talked his father into going pheasant hunting, then had proceeded to moon around, brooding as they followed the bird dog through the fields. He hadn't shot anything, not that he could hit the broadside of a barn—he hadn't gone hunting since he was a teenager—but he hadn't even raised the gun. Finally his dad had sat him down on a fallen log and dragged the whole story out of him.

He felt a little better having gotten it off his chest, but nothing much had changed. As soon as he got home he dashed to Kelsie's house with a box of devil's-food cupcakes and an apology for having acted like a bastard. She had forgiven him, then run off to the Cub Scout meeting with Jeffrey. Their only contact since then had been stilted conversations over the phone.

He was going to have to bide his time with her. Those words were just as true coming from Bud McKnight's mouth as they had been coming from Alec's own. Kelsie had told him straight off she didn't have time for a relationship; he had no right to throw a tantrum about it now. Her world wasn't going to come to a grinding halt because Alec McKnight was suddenly in love with her.

She loves me, too, he reminded himself. She had told him so. Somehow, that knowledge didn't console him the way it should have. It didn't quiet the fear that she was never going to find time for them to be together.

Forcing his attention to the work on his desk, Alec shook his head. Of all the ideas his staff had presented him for the new Van Bryant campaign, he was still hanging on to Steve Randall's Darwin the chimp idea—not because he liked it, but because of Kelsie. He wanted to help her because he loved her. He hated to see her working day and night, hated to see her worrying about bills. At the same time, it went against him to include the Darwin idea in what he was about to show Van Bryant. He didn't think it was the right approach for the store's campaign. He didn't think it was right for him to include it simply because he was in love with the chimp's agent.

Or did it all really come down to the possibility that he was afraid, a little voice asked him. He sat up straight and stiff in his chair at the thought, his shoulders squared defensively, a scowl on his face. The little voice was undaunted. Wasn't he really afraid Van Bryant would like the idea, and Kelsie would leave him in the dust once he wasn't useful to her anymore? Just like Vena had.

The truth at last, he thought, thoroughly disgusted with himself.

He would include Steve Randall's ideas with the rest. The ultimate decision was Eugene Van Bryant's to make anyway.

"I'm sorry, Alec," Mr. Van Bryant said, shaking his head gravely. He motioned to the campaign ideas Alec had shown him thus far. "These don't do it for me."

Alec couldn't keep his eyes from straying to the new Mrs. Van Bryant, who had accompanied her husband to learn more about the business. It was doubtful Eugene said anything like that about *her*. Van Bryant's junior by a good thirty years, Krissie was a doe-eyed brunette with an incredible body poured into a baby-blue knit dress. Rumor—and the rest of the Van Bryant clan—claimed the young woman was a gold digger. Alec reserved judgment. Eugene was no toad. There was something reminiscent of Cary Grant in the older man's distinguished looks. Who was to say the old guy couldn't hook a looker like Krissie? Love, as Alec was discovering, was a very funny business.

"I'm not saying they aren't good ideas," Van Bryant continued. "I just feel it's time for something really different for us. I'm sick of Van Bryant's being considered a snobby store. While Krissie and I were in Europe, I decided the time has come for a change for Van Bryant Department Stores. Change is what keeps us young. I know the rest of the family disagrees with me about the new image, but to hell with them; I'm still in charge here. I want Van Bryant's to be young, trendy, in a word—fun."

Alec's head lifted a fraction. He gave Van Bryant his most engaging grin. "Then you'll want to take a look at this last idea I have here for you, Mr. Van Bryant. How do you feel about chimpanzees?"

The phone rang as Kelsie fed the last of the rabbits. Her heart bolted at the thought that it could be Alec. After trying to call him a hundred times since they had parted on such a bad note, she had grown to know and hate his answering machine but had come no closer to mending the rift between them. Then he had shown up on her doorstep with a box of cupcakes, an apology, and a smile that made the first two items completely unncessary.

Honestly—Kelsie shook her head as she crossed the basement to the phone on her desk—when Alec got within arm's length of her and smiled that smile, it was like being put under hypnosis. She would have forgiven him anything, would have done anything for him.

She snatched the receiver up with a breathless greeting.

"Is this Monkey Business?" a man's voice asked.

"Yes, it is," she said, disappointed it wasn't Alec and angry with herself for it. She needed the business; she should have been ecstatic.

"Great. Listen, we've got this bachelor party Friday night, and monkey business is just what we've got in mind, if you know what I mean," he said with a lascivious chuckle.

Kelsie heaved a sigh and sank down onto her squeaky desk chair. "This isn't *that* kind of business."

"You don't show up at parties and dance around and take your clothes off?"

"Not if my life depended upon it. Good-bye." Recradling the receiver, it occurred to her she should have tried to get the man to hire Darwin the chimp. Darwin could have entertained the troops by throwing lingerie around and swinging from the drapes. She shook her head. "You're really stooping low, Kelsie. Low. Reptile's belly-on-the-ground low."

It was a sign of her nervousness about the coming months. While her Christmas-season bookings were respectable, with clients hired out for parties and pageants and sleigh rides at area shopping malls, January and February were virtually empty. As she thought about what her heating bills were going to be for those same months, premature chills ran through her.

The phone rang again and she lifted the receiver, hoping there would be a legitimate job prospect on the other end of the line.

"Kelsie Connors."

"Is this the Kelsie Connors with the sexy eyebrows?"

Suddenly she felt as if she were cocooned in sun-warmed silk. "Alec." She could see his smile and lake-blue eyes as clearly as if he were right there in her basement.

"How'd you know it was me?" he asked. "You must get dozens of calls like that every day."

"As a matter of fact, I did just get a call requesting I dance around and take my clothes off at a bachelor party."

"What?" he sat up in his chair, distinctly

displeased at the idea of some other guy making suggestions like that to Kelsie.

"A misunderstanding. That's what I get for coming up with a name like Monkey Business. What's up?"

Alec gave her a wicked chuckle. "How can you ask me a question like that after talking about dancing around and taking your clothes off?"

"Al-ec!" she said with a groan, blushing like a teenager.

"Can you get away for lunch?" he asked, crossing his fingers. "It's business."

"Business? The kind that pays money?"

"You bet."

"What is it?"

"Ah! It's a surprise. Can you be at my office by eleven-thirty?"

Kelsie took deep breaths as she rode the elevator up toward the offices of Glendenning Advertising. She was nervous—a good kind of nervous—about the business Alec wanted to talk about. She was nervous about seeing Alec. They

had made up—if it really could be called that—
but they were still stepping around each other like
cats walking on eggshells. At least they had been
before his phone call this morning. It wasn't anything obvious, just a sensation she had that
wouldn't leave no matter how many times she pictured his smile. His anger had hung a wall between them, a thin, invisible wall, but a wall just
the same.

She had warned him, she thought defensively.
She had said she didn't have time in her life for an
affair. There were already so many demands on
her time, and now part of her wanted to chuck it
all and live only for Alec. That terrified her. She
couldn't let herself fall into a dependent relationship again. She should never have let him talk her
into dating him.

"As if I had a choice," she grumbled to herself.
The guy could have made a million bucks as a
door-to-door salesman. Certainly there wasn't a
woman on the planet who wouldn't have melted at
the sight of his wily smile. And when he set his
mind to something, there was no changing it. The
combination of his cut-from-granite determination

and all-American-rascal charm was lethal. He could have sold sports cars to the Amish. "You never stood a chance, Kelsie."

Now she was in love with him, and the knowledge caused her more fear than anything else. She hadn't known anything about dating. She wasn't sure she knew much more about love. Part of what she had felt for her ex-husband had been love, but it had been so intermingled with dependence, with fear of the unknown, and it had been destroyed so long ago. . . .

The opening of the elevator doors stole away any more time she might have given to brooding.

Ms. Bond ushered her into Alec's office. Alec's face was alight with suppressed mischief. Smiles he refused to give rein to tugged at his lips as he looked from Kelsie to his secretary. "Thank you, Mr. Bond. Why don't you take off for lunch now?"

Ms. Bond's eyebrows scaled her forehead. "It's only eleven-thirty."

"Treat yourself. Ms. Connors and I will be taking a long lunch, so there's no need for you to hurry back. Two should be early enough."

"Would this be a good time to ask for a raise?" Ms. Bond questioned.

"Don't push your luck, Ms. Bond," he said through his teeth.

"Har!" She laughed, leaving the room.

"Have a seat, Ms. Connors," Alec told Kelsie with the formality of a little boy playing business executive. He motioned her to one of the chairs in front of his desk as he took his own seat.

Kelsie sat down, her nerves settling at Alec's obvious good mood. She crossed her legs and folded her hands on the lap of her green dress, looking at Alec expectantly.

His body tightened with need. She was so pretty sitting there with her attention solely on him, her big blue eyes watching him. She wore her hair loose, which suddenly drove him crazy with desire; it looked so soft and wild falling around her shoulders. His fingers itched to run through it, then undo the big brass buttons that marched down the front of her dress. Would she be wearing something sexy underneath? Something lacy he could play with?

A little uncomfortable at seeing the hot look in

Alec's eyes, Kelsie cleared her throat delicately. "You said something about business?"

"You got the Van Bryant deal," he said without preamble.

Kelsie's jaw dropped. "For real? You mean it? You're not suddenly into sick jokes, are you?" Mentally she was already paying off bills and picking out extra Christmas presents for the kids.

Alec laughed. "It's for real," he said, his heart warming at the thought that he had been able to make Kelsie look so happy.

"That's great! That's wonderful! That's—" She leaned back in her chair, suddenly wary of her good fortune.

"What?" Alec asked, seeing her swift change of mood.

She took a breath, holding it as she briefly stared down at her feet. "Um...did this have anything to do with us?" she asked quietly.

"I don't understand," Alec said, watching her.

"You didn't decide to give the idea a second chance because of you and me, did you? Because if the only reason I'm getting this job is...I know you're my number-one rescuer, Alec, but I couldn't accept that kind of favor. My business has to survive on merit, not on the good deeds of a knight in shining armor."

Alec's smile was an ironic one. He gave his head a little shake, dislodging a lock of neatly combed, dark hair so it tumbled roguishly across his forehead. Vena had not only expected such favors from him, she had demanded them on more than one occasion.

"What?" Kelsie asked, bewildered.

"Nothing," he said, his smile gentling for her as he pushed his chair back and stood. "The ultimate decision was Mr. Van Bryant's to make. He simply, flat-out loved the idea. It was exactly what he wanted. Congratulations."

"That's fabulous." She sighed, her eyes drifting shut for a moment. The image of the teal blue silk dress she'd had her eye on in Van Bryant's front window shimmered in her mind. "The timing couldn't have been better. Have you told Steve?"

"Yes. He wanted to take you out for a celebratory

lunch, but I had to tell him you were already booked."

He held his arms out for her. It seemed like the most natural thing in the world for Kelsie to go to him. She beamed a smile up at him. "So where are you taking me?"

"I don't see any reason to leave this room," he said as his arms tightened around her. "I have what I'm hungry for right here."

Kelsie giggled. "Alec! We're in your office!"

"Mmm, I know," he whispered, nuzzling behind her ear. "Do you have any idea how many times I've dreamed of making love to you in here?"

"No," she said, gasping as his palm brushed over her breast.

"Thousands," he said, nibbling at the corner of her mouth. He gave her a teasing kiss, dipping his tongue in to touch hers, then withdrawing. As he sifted her hair through his hands, he kissed her eyebrows, traced their slight arc with the tip of his tongue, grazed them with his teeth. "You have the sexiest eyebrows."

Kelsie had never considered her eyebrows an erogenous zone until now. Alec made love to them with his mouth, setting off a trembling sensation that raced down her body and settled between her thighs. She tried to wiggle away from him, managing only to worsen the situation as she came into more intimate contact with his aroused body.

"Alec, stop trying to seduce me," she said with no authority in her voice at all. Her resolve had gone as weak as her knees.

"Why?" he asked, chuckling deviously.

"Because you're so darn good at it!" Kelsie answered, knowing she shouldn't give in to him here but knowing she would. She had no kind of control when Alec touched her.

His fingers went to the top button of her dress, freeing it and then to two of its companions below. "Let's see if you're wearing something sexy for me, sweetheart," he said, easing the dress back off her shoulders.

A purr of satisfaction rumbled low in his throat, and he smiled as he uncovered her. The camisole she wore was pearly pink satin with a panel of sheer ivory lace down the center. Tiny pearl buttons drew a line from between her breasts downward, disappearing into the belted waist of her dress. He unfastened them with ease.

"Alec, we shouldn't." Even as she uttered the puny protest, Kelsie's thumbs hooked under Alec's red suspenders and began tugging them off his shoulders. "We're in your office; anybody could walk in."

"They've all gone to lunch," he said, maneuvering Kelsie so she was half sitting on his desk, the narrow skirt of her dress riding high up her thighs. He ran his hands up her legs as he lowered his head toward her breast.

A brisk rapping on his office door jerked Alec's head up.

"Alec, you home?"

Alec swore swiftly and eloquently. Kelsie scrambled from the desktop, wildly looking around for a place to hide.

"Under the desk!" Alec ordered in a frantic whisper. Before Kelsie could protest, he planted a hand on top of her head and shoved. The next thing she knew, she was on her fanny in the cubbyhole on Alec's desk, staring at a pair of gray argyle socks and black and gray wingtip shoes.

Alec dropped into his chair just as the door opened and Art Parnell stuck his balding head in. "Art, come on in."

Parnell was a small, chubby fellow with a footlong lock of black hair he combed from the right side of his head over the top.

"Here are those figures you wanted—jeez, you look like hell," the man said, taking a seat in front of Alec's desk.

"Do I?" Alec was still breathing hard, his face was flushed, and his tie was askew. He raked a hand back through the disheveled mass of his hair, trying vainly to restore a modicum of order to it. Hoping to look nonchalant, he shrugged his suspenders back into place.

"You're a slave to this place, Alec. You work too hard. I've got just the thing for you," the little man said, his beady eyes gleaming. "There's this little redhead in the mailroom who'll really deliver, if you get my drift—"

"I don't think so, Art," Alec interrupted. The

last thing he wanted right now was one of Art's never-ending play-by-play accounts of his disgusting extracurricular activities. "I'm seeing someone."

"Not often enough by the look of you." Parnell chuckled.

Under the desk Kelsie made a face. What a vulgarian! And, while Alec's answering laugh was less then halfhearted, she was none too pleased with him either. He'd been awfully quick to stuff her into this convenient little spot. Now she had a hole the size of Vermont in her panty hose and her neck was beginning to cramp.

"You've been spending too much time looking at that secretary of yours. Man, her face belongs on a wrestling poster! Do you believe what she said to me when I made that suggestion for the Christmas party? I've got nothing against women with brains—as long as they've got plenty of T and A to go along with it! Right?"

While Parnell laughed at his own tasteless joke, Alec gave him the same sort of pained, tight-lipped smile he gave his dentist.

"You ought to dump that old broad and get a sportier model, if you know what I mean."

"Oh, I couldn't get rid of Ms. Bond," Alec said. Suddenly his breath lodged in his throat. The look on his face was one of near pain.

"You okay?"

"F-fine," he stuttered, drumming his knuckles against the top of his desk, while underneath it Kelsie had decided to take advantage of the situation. "It's j-just a—a muscle spasm. Must have—a-strained something running."

"Running." Art grimaced, patting his paunch lovingly. "I get all the strain I need in the sack."

"G-good for you," Alec said hoarsely, squirming on his chair. Short of reaching under the desk—which would have been a little conspicuous—there wasn't anything he could do to stop Kelsie from her little game. He wasn't so sure he wanted her to stop. What he wanted was for Art Parnell to make himself scarce. "You know, now that you mention it, I'm not feeling too well, Art. You'd better leave. It's probably the stomach flu."

Parnell shot out of his chair. "I just had it," he

said, backing toward the door. "Cripes, I lived in the bathroom for two days. You'd better lie down or something, Alec."

"Oh..." he said in a soprano voice as Kelsie's fingers moved on his thigh. "I will. Right away. Good-bye, Art."

As soon as Art was out the door, Alec bolted across the room to lock it.

"Kelsie Connors," he said with a growl, half laughing as he stalked toward the desk, "you little witch. I'm going to get you for that stunt."

Kelsie stayed put under the desk, holding her stomach, laughing. "Maybe you should just go down to the mailroom, Alec."

He muttered his opinion of that suggestion as he dropped down on his knees and reached under the desk to drag Kelsie out. She pretended to struggle, giggling as he tickled her. Alec hauled her up off the floor and into his arms, kissing her wildly. He hugged her against his chest, and gave free run to the desire that had been building inside him.

What was left of Kelsie's control dissolved, and

she kissed him back, groaning as he brought one hard thigh up between hers, inviting her to arch against him. The hunger she felt for him was overwhelming. Every cell of her body ached for his touch. The first time she had felt this kind of need it had frightened her. Now what she felt was a ravenous sense of anticipation, because she knew Alec could satisfy her hunger and leave her feeling exalted instead of empty.

She jerked his suspenders down and went for his tie, her hands fumbling frantically until she nearly choked him. Alec jerked the strip of silk from his shirt collar and dropped it on his desk, hurrying his mouth back to Kelsie's for another kiss. His need for her was beyond anything he'd ever known. They were like fire and dynamite when they came together. He wondered if Kelsie realized how rare that kind of explosive mutual passion was.

Buttons flew off his shirt as her hands sought to touch his chest. Her dress pooled at her waist. Alec bent her back over his desk, his mouth closing hotly over a breast, while his hands chased her skirt up and yanked hose and panties down.

Kelsie braced a foot on the arm of the desk chair, lifting her hips to Alec's touch, moving in time to the rhythm his boldly teasing fingers set.

Giving herself over to the tidal wave of sensation that engulfed her, Kelsie lay back on the desk, writhing and moaning until she didn't think she could stand much more pleasure. She tugged on Alec's hair, dragging his head up. Her breasts were gleaning, her nipples swollen and red.

"Alec," she said with a gasp, her pulse racing.

He pulled her up, claiming her mouth once again as Kelsie's hands went to the waistband of his pants. They groaned into each other's mouths as her hand closed around him. Alec's hand settled over her and silently taught her how he liked to be stroked, a lesson that was short-lived as his need raced out of control.

They raced toward fulfillment, reaching it together. Alec caught Kelsie's soft, wild cries of completion in his mouth. He strained against her, her body holding him deep inside as wave after wave of unbelievable pleasure tightened her around him.

Finally Kelsie relaxed, laying on the desk. She smiled up at him as he leaned over her. They were both panting as if they'd just run the New York marathon. Alec smiled back. She looked like a centerfold model, sprawled on his desk with her dress still belted around her waist, her breasts beautifully bare.

His desk looked as if it had been ransacked. There were papers everywhere, the mug that held pens and pencils had overturned, as had his coffee cups. Now there was a small puddle of coffee soaking into yesterday's *Wall Street Journal,* and his lamp was dangling over the edge of the desk by its cord. It was the kind of mess that normally would have made him nauseated. At the moment he couldn't have cared less.

"I love you," he whispered as he unbuckled the wide leather belt at Kelsie's waist. He unbuttoned the two buttons that held her dress together and opened the garment wide, bending over to press soft kisses to her tummy.

"I love you," he whispered again, gathering her into his arms to kiss her mouth.

"I love you," she whispered back.

With the initial urgency past, she closed her eyes and simply enjoyed the feel of his body against hers as he held her to him. But as it had their first night together, their desire returned in a hurry. Kisses grew hungrier, touches more demanding. Kelsie couldn't stop thinking how wonderfully erotic it was to be totally naked in Alec's office.

"Alec," she cried, her body moving against his in a subtle caress. "I've never needed like this before."

"Me either," he said, his body clearly demonstrating just how much he needed her. He held Kelsie close, one hand stroking down the smooth, beautiful curve of her back. "This is special, honey. Most people never find what we have together."

He stood back and methodically shucked shoes, socks, and slacks, then took Kelsie by the hand and led her away from the desk. They stretched out on the soft, thick carpet in front of the cordovan leather sofa, kissing and touching. Alec moved to kneel between Kelsie's thighs, lifting her hips and joining their bodies once again. They made love slowly, taking each other to the edge, but always pulling back, prolonging the pleasure.

In the end, Alec took control. With one hand he parted the soft, swollen petals of feminine flesh and stroked her with the lightest of touches, setting off an avalanche of feelings. With eyes full of love and the shadows of desperation, he watched her face as ecstasy claimed her. When she had stilled beneath him, he held her tenderly and found his own completion.

They helped each other dress—a curiously sweet, quiet endeavor.

Kelsie still felt naked, even with all her clothes on. Her body was humming with awareness. Every nerve ending had become hypersensitive. She had a business meeting in less than an hour, and all she could think of was curling up in bed beside Alec for the rest of the day.

Dangerous. The word was like a thin cloud of smoke ribboning through the corridors of her mind. It appeared out of nowhere to send a sharp stab of fright through her but vanished when she tried to examine it and find its origin. It was never far from her mind, but she could never get hold of it. All she knew for certain was the more she loved Alec, the more that word came to mind, and the more frightened she became.

NINE

"WHAT NOW?" ALEC muttered to himself as he drove past Kelsie's house. The place was ablaze with lights. He had to go halfway down the block before he could find a parking spot. If this was some kind of party, he wasn't in the mood. He was beat. On top of putting in extra hours at the office trying to get everything ready to shoot the first series of ads for Van Bryant's, he'd been spending as much time as he could insinuating himself into Kelsie's life.

His plan was to show her A: that he was truly

interested in her life, and B: that all her little clubs and causes were not going to provide her with excuses to escape the serious relationship they were building—or would be building as soon as she decided the world could run without her constant supervision.

He hadn't missed one of Jeffrey's youth hockey games. He had watched Elizabeth master a double-toe loop in skating class. He had bravely volunteered to take a sick cat to the vet—he still had the claw marks to prove it. He had joined the Humane Society and had volunteered to speak at a Junior Achievers meeting. Still he wasn't seeing more of Kelsie, not in the way he wanted to.

It didn't make any sense at all. Since they had admitted their love for each other it seemed as though she had been avoiding him. She said she wanted to spend more time with him, but it wasn't happening. Of course it was the Christmas season, which complicated everyone's schedule. Maybe that was the problem.

Alec had tried taking his own advice, and his father's, about biding his time with Kelsie. The trouble was, he wasn't by nature a patient man.

He was used to setting a goal, then bulldozing over whatever he had to to reach that goal. He didn't seem to be making any headway in this situation, and he was beginning to feel frustrated and a little desperate.

The time for patience was over. If he had to drag her kicking and screaming, he was going to get Kelsie away from her thousand and one responsibilities for a couple of days of peace and quiet. They would go somewhere out of the way, have a serious discussion about their future together, and spend the rest of the time making love.

Jeffrey answered the door wearing his Cub Scout uniform and a paper-maché hat shaped like a brontosaurus. "Hi, Alec. We're making gingerbread men. Mine looks like Pee Wee Herman."

"That's great, sport. Is your mom around?"

"Sure."

Kelsie stepped into the open doorway, and Jeff ducked under her arm to return to the scout project in the kitchen. "Alec, what are you doing here?"

"What's going on?" he demanded, ignoring her question, annoyed that they obviously weren't going to be alone.

"The Cub Scouts' Christmas party. Didn't I tell you it was tonight?"

"Who knows," he grumbled. "I'd need to hire another secretary if I were going to keep track of every blessed meeting and party of yours."

Kelsie had just about had it with his little digs about her schedule. She'd *warned* him. She reached for the door as if she meant to close it in his face. "I'm busy right now, Alec. Maybe you could come back later to be rude and obnoxious."

Alec closed his eyes and forced a sigh. His attitude was getting him nowhere. He stuck an arm out to hold the door back. "I'm sorry. It's been a long day. Honey, if we can just talk for five minutes—"

"Alec, I don't have five minutes right now," Kelsie said, wincing as a crash sounded behind her. "Mothers are outnumbered twelve to two in the kitchen."

"Please, sweetheart." He tried to give her his best sincere look, but she was glancing over her shoulder at the little boys running around the dining room. "Kelsie, it's important," he said, exasperated by all the interruptions. "We need to talk."

"Will it still be important in three hours, when everyone is gone?" she asked, irritated by his impatience.

Alec knew he was being unreasonable, but for some reason it was important to him that they talk now, right now. He wanted her to drop everything so he could beg her to run away with him for the weekend. Maybe he was losing his mind, he reflected as he pushed past her into the living room. He clamped a cold hand around her wrist and started leading her down the hallway away from the sounds of imminent disaster in the kitchen. Maybe he was having an early midlife crisis. Next he'd be dying his hair and taking hang gliding lessons.

"Alec!" Kelsie protested, trying to dig her heels into the carpet. "I have guests."

"They can wait five minutes. I can't."

He steered her into her bedroom. Without even letting go of Kelsie, he shut the door and backed her against it. Her eyes were as big as moons as she stared at the fierce, determined expression on his face.

He looked a little wild, not at all like the coolheaded young executive. His usually neat hair spilled across his forehead. His dark, straight brows were lowered ominously over blazing blue eyes. Without the smile Kelsie had come to know and love, his finely chiseled mouth had an almost cynical twist to it. It struck her again what a contrast there was in Alec. He wasn't always the easygoing charmer. He could be formidable.

She had to wonder if he had finally realized she'd been right all along—that there just wasn't any way for them to have a normal relationship. She'd been waiting for this moment, but she was hardly ready. Her heart ached so, she wanted to turn away from him, but the intensity of his stare held her in place.

After a tense, itchy moment of silence, Alec took a deep breath and said, "Run away with me."

"What?" Kelsie laughed, relief leaving her so weak she couldn't have moved away from the door because she would have folded up like an accordion.

"I mean it, Kelsie. Run away with me this weekend. I've got a nice secluded little spot all picked out. It's a place we can go to and relax. We need some time alone together, honey."

A whole weekend with no interruptions for them to get their relationship on firmer footing? Kelsie found the prospect dangerously inviting. They were in love. They deserved a little quality time with each other, but...But what, Kelsie, she asked herself as warning tremors ran through her. Something about it scared her.

"I agree, we do need to get away," she said, stalling for time. "But this weekend is the Christmas bazaar for the Humane Society."

"So?" he asked.

"So I should be there. I'm the vice-president. I had to line up the horses for the sleigh rides and the animals for the live nativity scene—"

"Which you've done," Alec pointed out. "Your job is finished. There's no reason you have to be there."

"But someone should be there to make sure everything goes all right—"

"Call the chairperson and delegate it."

"But—"

"Kelsie, why are you trying so damn hard to find an excuse? If you'd rather spend the weekend with the Humane Society than with me, then maybe we don't need to discuss our relationship any further. I was under the mistaken impression that we were both in love—"

"We are!" she insisted, flustered. "I mean, I am—I mean, I do love you, Alec. It's just that this weekend is a bad time—"

He had a very explicit opinion of the Humane Society's claim on their weekend, which he muttered half under his breath.

"What about you?" she questioned, trying to turn the tables. "You've been swamped trying to get everything lined up for next week. How can you get away?"

"*I* delegated. They gave a great class on it at college—Delegating 101. Maybe you could audit it next semester, if you can handle the idea that the world can run without you being in charge of every blasted committee."

"What kind of crack is that?" she asked, planting her hands on her hips.

"Oh, I don't know," he said sarcastically as his shoulders moved in an exaggerated shrug. "I guess it's the kind I usually make when the woman I love is doing everything she can to sabotage our relationship."

"I am not!" Kelsie denied vehemently, wondering in the back of her mind why she felt she should have crossed her fingers before saying that.

"Then tell the Humane Society to take a flying leap, and say you'll come away with me this weekend." Both his tone and his look softened as he gazed down at her. He raised a hand to her cheek, stroking the downy softness with the backs of his fingers. "Please, honey. We have to make time for what's important. The Humane Society is a worthy cause, but so are we—you and I. We deserve this. We need it. I need you."

He was vulnerable. She could see it. He made no attempt to hide it. Way down deep in those ocean-blue eyes he looked as scared as she felt. It made her love him even more than she already did.

She needed him, too, but she couldn't say it. When her marriage had ended, Kelsie had vowed she would never let herself fall into the trap of being dependent on a man again. She couldn't need Alec, but she did, and part of her wanted to.

She loved him. Could need and dependence be separated from love?

"We do need this, don't we?" she said, looking down at her feet. Maybe she could sort out some of her own feelings while they were away. "What about the kids? I'm not sure I can find someone to stay with them for a whole weekend."

"I've already talked to my cousin Natalie. She's got no problem with staying the whole weekend. Her husband is an intern; he's going to be at the hospital."

"She's a law student and he's a doctor? That must be a rough schedule."

"Yeah," Alec agreed, his gaze holding hers. "And they're making it." He watched Kelsie shift uncomfortably, and swiftly lightened his mood. He was lucky his strong-arm tactics hadn't gotten him tossed out in the snow on his keister. He gave her a wily, bedimpled grin. "I can't wait to get you all to myself for a whole weekend."

It was remarkable. She was a grown woman with two children, she was this man's lover, for heaven's sake, and still he could make her blush. Hollywood would have laid the world at his feet for the chance to put his brand of sexual magnetism on the silver screen. There was no getting around it, Alec McKnight had a reservoir of charm as deep as Lake Superior, and eyes as blue, and Kelsie could scarcely look at him without feeling as if she were drowning.

She smiled at him and shook her head in disbelief at her body's response to him. "Where are we going?" she asked, resigning herself to the fact that Alec almost always managed to get his own way.

"La Croix House—a very special, very private inn that overlooks the Ste. Croix river. You'll love it."

"What should I pack? Ski clothes?"

"No." He smiled secretively.

"Evening clothes?"

"No." His smile widened. By rights, Kelsie thought, there should have been canary feathers sticking to his chin.

"What, then?"

"Remember that briefcase you brought to my office the day we met?" He bobbed his eyebrows at her as she blushed in remembrance of the lacy underthings in the attaché. "Bring that."

"What else?" she asked, fighting a losing battle against embarrassment.

Alec went right on grinning. "Your tooth-brush."

La Croix House was everything Alec had told her and then some, Kelsie thought as they turned in at the gate and started up the long, winding driveway. The early dusk of Minnesota winter was falling on the snow-blanketed fields, but amber lights cast a welcoming glow in the tall windows of the inn. The house was an enormous Greek revival style mansion, white with neat black shutters. Four Dorian columns rose gracefully to the top of the second story to support the wide roof of the portico. The main entrance boasted oak double doors with a wreath on each and a huge fanlight above them. In the spirit of the season, red ribbon and evergreen roping adorned the post where the sign hung welcoming them to La Croix House. Behind the house the land rose sharply into wooded hills that were black now in the gloom of twilight. The lawn in front of the house gradually sloped downhill. The frozen expanse of the Ste. Croix River lay below.

Alec parked the car, shut off the engine, and turned to give Kelsie an expectant smile. "Well?"

"It's beautiful, Alec," she murmured, feeling suddenly choked up because no one had ever taken her to such a special place. She tried humor to keep her tears at bay. "What can I say except you'd better not be considered a regular here."

He chuckled, not missing the sparkle of tears Kelsie had hastily blinked away. Reaching out to tuck a stray strand of blond hair behind her ear, he said, "I have been here exactly once. Post-divorce R and R," he explained. "It was just me, my skis, and a stack of Agatha Christie novels."

Kelsie leaned over and kissed him. "Let's go in before we freeze."

"I can think of several ways for us to stay warm," Alec said, his voice eager with suggestion.

"Hold those thoughts until we get to our room, will you?"

They were greeted in the foyer by a woman who was short and plump and had a smile that lit up her whole face.

"Hi! Welcome back, Alec." She laughed at the look of astonishment he gave her. "I never forget a name or a recipe for fattening food. The one trait comes in handy, the other goes straight to my hips," she said with a rueful smile. Reaching out to shake Kelsie's hand, she said, "You must be Kelsie. I'm Ann Lancaster. Welcome to La Croix House."

"Thank you," Kelsie said, liking the woman instantly. "The house is beautiful."

"Thank you. We're very proud of it. My husband and son and I have done most of the restoration work ourselves. I'll give you a mini tour, then take you up to your room."

The tour of the house would have been worth paying admission for. Each room had been lovingly restored, from the polished wood floors to the ornate moldings and plasterwork on the high ceilings. Oriental rugs graced the floors. The furnishings were antiques. All of the first floor rooms that were open to guests—the two parlors, library, and large dining room—had been decorated for Christmas with evergreen bows and sprigs of holly, wreaths, baskets of pine cones, and velvet and taffeta ribbons.

The seven guest rooms, Mrs. Lancaster explained as they climbed the curving staircase, had been decorated with luxury in mind ahead of historical accuracy. The furnishings were still antiques, but the floors were covered with lush carpeting and each room had its own Jacuzzi.

On the door to the room Alec had reserved for them, a small hand-lettered sign read:

Alec and Kelsie
Peace and Quiet for a Whole Weekend!
Enjoy!

When the door closed behind them, Alec set the suitcases down, sighed, and stretched his arms and shoulders, ready to relax. Conversely, Kelsie seemed to tense up. Not that she'd been overly relaxed on the drive. She had fidgeted and chewed her lip the whole way. She hadn't said a word about it, but Alec knew something about this weekend was bothering her. She was as easy to read as a billboard.

"Would you care to discuss it?" he asked, watching her prowl around the room.

Her head jerked around in his direction. "What?"

Alec gave her a tiny smile. "Whatever it is that's making you so nervous when you're supposed to be unwinding."

"Oh," she said in a small voice. Why did she have to be as transparent as plastic wrap, she wondered. At least she didn't have to lie to him. There were a dozen things making her nervous; all she had to do was pick one that didn't involve him. She shrugged, stuffing her hands into the pockets of her jeans. "It's just that...I've never left the kids for a whole weekend before, and..." As she dodged Alec's penetrating gaze, her eyes landed on the telephone sitting beside a thriving Boston fern on a pine dry sink. "Maybe I should call to make sure—"

Alec shook his head, smiling indulgently. He came forward to gently brush her hair back from her face and press a sweet kiss to her lips. "Natalie has this number. She'll call if anything really important happens, such as terrorists taking them hostage or a nuclear bomb hitting your house."

"I know. But Elizabeth had a dentist appointment today."

Alec frowned. "Drilling? Filling? Pulling?"

"Just a checkup," she said, feeling ridiculous.

To his credit, Alec didn't laugh, but he tried to get Kelsie to. "That ranks somewhere below a neo-Nazi uprising. Close, mind you, but not quite as bad."

She cracked a pathetic excuse for a smile.

"Honey, they'll be fine," he assured her, taking her in his arms.

Kelsie's shoulders slumped in defeat. "Yeah." She sighed, giving in to the urge to put her arms around Alec's lean waist and snuggle against him.

It helped to be closer to him, but it didn't chase away the hollow sense of panic inside her. She shouldn't have come here with him. She should never have let him talk her into it. Of course, it would have been easier to walk to the moon than resist Alec's powers of persuasion. All her hard-won independence became as soft as Silly Putty when she went up against Alec's granite-willed, velvet-cloaked determination.

She was becoming dependent on him. That was

the bottom line. That was what really scared her. He had worked his way into her life and made himself indispensable. He was always there for her in times of crisis, her knight in shining armor, inviting her to lean on him. How could she deny him anything?

Why did love have to be so complicated? She couldn't give in to the temptation of becoming emotionally dependent on him. She had been totally dependent on Jack and it had nearly destroyed her. She would never forget the raw terror that had permeated ever fiber of her being when she had realized Jack was never going to be there for her again, that she was essentially alone. No one would ever know the struggle she had gone through to become self-sufficient, to take charge of her life. If she had to go through it again, she wasn't so sure she would survive.

Why did love have to be so complicated? She loved Alec, but could she make him understand she had to have a life outside their relationship? He'd been doing everything he could to invade every corner of her existence. How was he going to react when she asked him to back off? She knew he wouldn't take it well. She didn't want to lose him, she just needed some space.

Why did love have to be so complicated?

"Come here," he said, stepping out of her embrace and drawing her with him toward the tall window, where a plump lavender velvet cushion beckoned them to make use of the window seat.

"We should get ready for dinner," Kelsie protested.

"It can wait," he said softly, sitting with his back against the wall of the alcove, one leg drawn up on the seat, the other foot on the floor. He pulled her down to sit in the vee of his legs with her back to his chest, and wrapped his arms around her. "Isn't this nice?"

She nodded automatically, not bothering to ask if he was referring to the room or the view or the quiet or them sitting together. Letting her gaze take in the details of their surroundings, she said, "This is like my all-time fantasy bedroom. Have you been reading my mind, Alec McKnight?"

He chuckled devilishly. "I'll never tell."

The room was light and larger than any two bedrooms in Kelsie's house. Dainty violet flowers and green vines entwined on the white background of the wallpaper. The carpet and drapes were silver-gray. There were actually two levels to the room. On the lower level, thick lavender towels sat in a wicker basket beside the gray marble Jacuzzi. Two delicate rosewood chairs and a small table covered in white lace sat not far from the window seat, where the morning sun and the view of the river would provide a lovely setting for an intimate breakfast. Several carpeted steps led up to a specious loft, where an ornate brass bed situated beneath a skylight was the main attraction and two comfortable-looking overstuffed chairs flanked a brass floor lamp.

Special touches added warmth and homeyness to both levels: dishes of sweet-smelling potpourri, lush green plants in hand-thrown pottery, satin and lace pillows, framed needlework, and wreaths made of baby's breath and grapevine adorning the walls.

It was a perfect haven. Kelsie felt guilty she hadn't been enjoying it and resolved not to let her brooding ruin their time here. She turned her gaze out the window to the moon-silvered evening, the ethereal glow of ice on the river, the pristine whiteness of snow on the fields.

"Too bad I don't know how to ski," she said, looking over her shoulder at Alec. "I bet they have some lovely cross-country trails here."

"They do, but you wouldn't have gotten to see them," he said, a smile threatening to spread across his face.

"Why not?"

"Because, sweetheart, I have no intention of letting you out of this room until checkout time." His true intentions burned like dark fires in his eyes.

Kelsie felt her body react immediately. It never ceased to amaze her how in tune they were physically. One look, one word from him, and everything inside her went into meltdown. "Alec," she whispered, arching back against him like a wanton cat, "you are wicked."

"Thoroughly," he agreed, lowering his mouth to hers for a deep, leisurely kiss.

He had no intention of making use of the elegant dining room downstairs. They had seen all of the rest of the inn they were going to see on the tour. Their dinner was delivered to their door, announced by a discreet ring of a small bell, and left in the hall on a serving cart.

"I arranged for all our meals to be brought to our room," he said, wheeling the cart to the table.

"Al-ec!" Kelsie said, mortified. "What will the Lancasters think? They'll think we came here only for—for—"

"We did," he said with a grin, dimples flashing as he pulled her into his arms. She had begun to change clothes to go downstairs, so her oversized chambray shirt was hanging loose and unbuttoned, revealing the top half of a lace-edged royal blue teddy. Alec dropped one knee to the seat of a chair and bent his head to nuzzle her barely concealed breast.

Kelsie melted into the heat of his mouth and reprimanded him all at once. "Alec, stop that. If we get sidetracked now, we'll never eat this meal, and the innkeepers will know why."

"Honey, I'm sure they have better things to do than wonder about the sexual habits of all their guests," he said, staring fascinated at the way her hardened nipple peeked at him through the lace of her teddy. "Why should it bother you anyway? We're consenting adults."

"Because," she said primly, "good Norwegian Lutheran girls aren't raised to run off with men for hanky-panky."

"Oh, really?" he asked dryly. He slipped the tip of his tongue inside the edge of her teddy and flicked it across the taught tip of her breast. "Then what are you doing here?"

She gasped. Of its own volition, one hand lifted to bare her breast for his sensual ministrations, and cup it to give him better access. Breathlessly she replied, "We're not immune to temptation."

"Praise be." Alec groaned against her soft, hot skin. He sucked her breast until she was moaning and withering in his arms, then he lifted his head and stood up, announcing in a cheery tone, "Dinnertime!"

Kelsie gave him a look that managed to combine disbelief, desperation, and a trace of humor. She shook a finger at him. "Just you wait, Alexander McKnight."

The devil himself couldn't have come up with a more suggestive smile than the one Alec gave her. "I am," he said, catching her hand and drawing it to the straining front of his jeans.

A thrill shot through Kelsie. He was denying them both for the moment, so their anticipation could build. If hers built much more, she was going to explode, she thought as she slumped down on the chair.

Dinner conversation was minimal, provided mainly by the occasional monologue of the radio announcer between segments of music on the classical station. Kelsie and Alec were too busy concentrating on each other and the sweet, hot tension thickening the air around them.

She found her attention drawn to his hands. They were well tended. Elegant. They were so finely shaped, they were nearly feminine. An artist's hands. Or a musician's. Thoughts of the beautiful music they could make on her body sent a rush of heat through her.

Alec couldn't take his eyes off her mouth. He could never get over how soft it looked—how soft it was. It was beautifully sculpted, not too wide or too small or too full or too thin. In short, it was the most kissable mouth he knew. Thoughts of how giving it was when he kissed it, how pliant and welcoming and warm and sweet it was beneath his, had him shifting uncomfortably on his chair.

They did little justice to the excellent meal of delicately seasoned wild duck on a bed of wild rice. The carafe of wine was emptied by half without either of them having tasted a drop.

When they gave up on the meal, Alec wheeled the tray with their dishes on it into the hall. He stepped back into the room, closed the door and locked it, then sauntered over to where Kelsie stood next to her chair watching him with wide eyes.

"Now," he said in a low, silky voice, lowering one knee to the chair as he had earlier. "If I remember right, we left off right about here."

He did indeed take up where he'd left off, lavishing attention on Kelsie's small, proud breasts. Deliberately closing her mind to anything else, Kelsie let passion fill her, let it flow from her in every touch as she caressed his strong shoulders and back. They could deal with the problems in their relationship later. Tonight she would love him with no reservations, without holding back. She would love him with her body and her soul, and pray that it would be enough.

They abandoned their clothes at the table where the candles from dinner had guttered and gone out. Alec led her to the softly lit alcove that housed the Jacuzzi, and they both sat on the edge of the sunken tub of churning water. He stepped down into the silky warmth, turning back toward Kelsie as if he meant to help her in, but when she started to slide forward, he stopped her with his hands on her knees.

"Alec?" she questioned softly.

His gaze intent on her face, he parted her thighs and stepped between them. "Lie back, sweetheart. Let me love you."

She did as he asked, leaning back, supporting herself with her hands as he bent his head. Gently his fingers opened her and he kissed her intimately, his mouth moving against her in a gentle, languid rhythm, his tongue stroking the essence of her. His name coursed through her brain, but Kelsie was uncertain she said it aloud. An inner fire was consuming her, roaring in her ears; flames of desire that were not extinguished by the waves of ecstasy pouring over her.

Then the intangible waves of sensation became

tangible waves of warm liquid. Alec drew her down into the tub with him, catching his lower lip between his teeth as his hardness penetrated her soft, tight warmth. He held her, his breath coming in sharp, staccato gasps, and watched her face, and knew a sudden panic deep in his chest.

"I love you." His voice was a gravel-edged rasp. "Love me, Kelsie," he pleaded.

"I do," she whispered, her gaze locked on the tortured expression he wore. "More than you know."

Later, they lay in the big brass bed, making love under the skylight, showered in the light of the moon and a million diamond-cut stars. Alec braced himself on his forearms, meeting the urgent thrusts of Kelsie's hips with slow, deep strokes. They found heaven together—a brilliant flash that made the stars above them pale in comparison—and Alec eased himself down on top of her and whispered so softly she almost didn't hear him, "Need me, Kelsie."

I do, she thought, holding him tight. More than I should.

TEN

"GOOD MORNING, BEAUTIFUL," a sleep-roughened voice said in her ear. Warm lips kissed her shoulder as a hand slipped over the curve of her hip to rub her tummy.

"Liar," Kelsie said, forcing a chuckle. "I know exactly what I look like in the morning—bad enough to scare Stephen King."

"Let me see," Alec said, turning her over on her back. "I've got a strong stomach."

"Very funny," she said, trying to push her mussed hair out of her face.

His smile changed to a look of concern as he traced a forefinger along the violet smudges beneath her eyes. "Didn't you sleep well?"

"As I recall, I was busy with other things most of last night," she answered. She hadn't slept at all, but had lain awake, her thoughts churning around and around until she'd given herself a headache.

Alec, on the other hand, looked remarkably well-rested and impossibly virile as he leaned over her. His dark hair tumbled roguishly onto his forehead, his morning beard shadowed his jaw. His mouth eased into a wide, lazy smile. "Oh, yeah. I remember."

He fell onto his back, pulling Kelsie into his arms so she snuggled beside him with her head in the hollow of his shoulder. "It felt so good to hold you all night," he said, kissing her hair. "We'll have to do this more often, right?"

"Right," she agreed with false conviction. He heard it, too, and started to sit up. Before he could question her, though, a bell sounded outside their door.

"Must be breakfast," Kelsie said brightly, popping out of bed. She threw on her white silk robe and belted it on the way to the door. "I don't know about you, but I'm famished."

She wheeled in a cart laden with platters of fresh fruit, eggs, and meats, and a stoneware crock full of steaming hot muffins. Vaguely acknowledging the wonderful aroma, she abandoned the cart to answer the telephone.

Alec watched her with wariness in his eyes as he climbed out of bed and tugged on a pair of gray sweat pants. This morning she didn't seem like the Kelsie he'd made love to most of the night. Barriers that had been nonexistent in the dark had been hastily resurrected before dawn. She was pulling away from him. Why?

Padding barefoot to the table to pour himself a cup of coffee, he listened with interest to her end of the telephone conversation.

"Yes, I realize that...yes...oh, dear...no... no, of course, I understand...right...just calm down...I'll be there as soon as I can."

"Jeffrey? Elizabeth?" he questioned, concern knitting his brows.

"The Humane Society."

Everything inside him went cold, then started boiling. "The what?"

Kelsie swallowed hard at the murderous look on his face. "The Humane—"

"I can't believe you gave them this phone number! Kelsie, how could you?"

"I had to, Alec. I'm the vice-president, and the bazaar—"

"Bazaar!" he exploded. "*Bizarre,* that's what this is! You let our weekend get interrupted for an update on a stupid bazaar?"

Kelsie glared at him, more than ready to vent some of her pent-up feelings. "It may not be important to you, Alec, but it's a cause I believe in—"

"And we're not?" he asked with an exaggerated shrug.

"Don't be absurd," she said. "Of course we are."

"Oh, really? Where did you just promise to be as soon as you can? With me?"

Now it's going to hit the fan, Kelsie thought, her whole body trembling in anticipation of something terrible. She felt as if they were being swept into dangerous flood waters, but were powerless to save themselves. "Mrs. Pollan-Ryan, the president, broke her hip playing broom ball last night, leaving no one in charge of the bazaar. I have to—"

"The hell you do," he interrupted in a dangerous voice. At that moment he looked like a very dangerous man, his muscled bare chest heaving, his eyes as cold and glittering as sapphires.

"Alec, I have to go back," she said.

"Why? Because you're sure there's no other person in the area that can handle it? Kelsie Connors, Superwoman, to the rescue, right?"

"Alec, I have to go back," she said, trying her best to keep her voice steady. "They need me."

He stood staring at her for a moment, his jaw working. Finally he said, "I need you too."

Kelsie pressed her eyes shut, then took a deep shaky breath and let it out. "Alec, don't do this."

"Don't what?" What was he doing? *She* was the one who was pushing them into dangerous territory, all for some ludicrous bazaar.

She glared at him through a sheen of tears. "We can come back here some other weekend." Why am I being so stubborn about this, she wondered in the back of her mind. It wasn't *that* important to her. Someone else probably could have done it, but she'd jumped at the chance as if she were afraid to be alone with Alec for another two days. Maybe she was.

"When?" he demanded. "Some weekend when there's nothing going on with the Humane Society or the League of Businesswomen or the Over-achievers or any of the myriad other groups you cling to?"

"Cling to?" she said with a gasp, hurt and anger warring inside her. "I warned you ahead of time, Alec. I told you I didn't have time, that I had responsibilities—"

"Responsibilities?" he questioned, his own hurt pushing him to say things he knew he shouldn't. "Did it ever occur to you that you spread yourself so thin working for all these ridiculous groups be-cause you're *afraid* of responsibility? You're afraid of the responsibility of committing yourself to a relationship. Your marriage flopped, and you're too much of a coward to risk finding hap-piness with a man. You join everything there is to join to fill up your empty life."

"That's a vicious thing to say!" she shouted, tears spilling down her cheeks.

"It's the damn truth!"

She turned away from him, angrily wiping at her tears, trying to get a handle on herself. Why did women always have to be the ones to cry during arguments? It wasn't fair.

Behind her, Alec planted his hands on his hips and heaved a sigh, cursing under his breath. She'd pushed him into saying it. Maybe it had been cruel, but it had needed to be said. He was sick of trying to coax her out her self-imposed exile. It was time she saw what she was doing to herself and made a decision one way or the other.

But what if she decided against him, he wondered. He loved her. He didn't want to lose her. He especially didn't want to lose her over such a trivial thing as this bazaar. It was ridiculous. But this weekend was important to him. He hadn't set out to make it a test of the depth of her feelings, but that was what it was turning into.

It made his stomach knot to think she was failing the test. He didn't want to lose her. He loved her. He needed her.

He needed her to need him too. She had to need him more than she needed the Humane Society.

"Kelsie," he said, his voice as raspy as a chain smoker's. "Call them back and tell them to get someone else."

She could hear "or else" ringing in her ears even though he hadn't said it. A Christmas bazaar. What a stupid thing to be fighting over, she thought. But it represented much more to her than a fund-raiser for a worthy cause. Alec had no idea how much courage it had taken for her to push aside her shyness and join those "ridiculous groups." When her marriage had ended, she had been so afraid. Becoming involved had been a big step in overcoming her fears. It had come to be a symbol of her independence.

What she heard him asking now was to choose between dependence and independence. If she gave up this small piece of her independence, wasn't he going to ask for more and more? They were lovers, nothing more. He hadn't talked about any kind of commitment between them; he'd made no promises. She hadn't asked for or expected any. She had no guarantee he wouldn't steal away her independence, then lose interest in her—like Jack had. She closed her eyes and remembered the fear and the cold emptiness, and knew she couldn't go through it again.

Without another word to Alec, she crossed the room to her suitcase.

He could have refused to drive her back, Alec thought as he piloted the car toward the Twin Cities with a heavy foot on the accelerator, but what purpose would it have served? He could have refused to take her directly to the site of the bazaar, but that would have been childish and petty. Of course, he reflected, his jaw clenched at a stubborn angle, a man deserved to be childish and petty after getting dumped, but he would rise above that. At least until he got home.

He couldn't believe Kelsie was ruining their weekend over a stupid Christmas bazaar. He couldn't believe they'd had such a dreadful fight over it. He couldn't believe he'd lost her because of it. It all seemed unreal.

But lost her he had, and it didn't come down to a benefit for homeless animals. It came down to the fact that she didn't need him. When it came to making time for what was important, his name wasn't at the top of her list. So it was probably just as well things had ended here. He'd already had his fill of relationships where he was nothing more than a convenience. He was tired of being the disposable McKnight in shining armor.

It would be a new year soon, a good time to start over. First he had to get through Christmas. He thought of the pearl necklace he'd bought Kelsie, reposing in its black velvet box in his sock drawer, and had to blink back a sudden mistiness in his eyes.

Kelsie crowded against the door on the passenger side of the car, a cramp in her neck from forcing herself to stare out the window so Alec wouldn't see the constant battle she was waging against tears. If she couldn't salvage anything else, she would try to salvage her pride. He'd said some ugly things to her. Maybe it was just as well their relationship was ending now, if he thought so little of her. She'd known from the start she shouldn't have gotten involved with him. If only she'd had some defense against the potent combination of his wily charm and winning smile.

She pressed a mutilated tissue under her nose and bit her lip as a new wave of depression swept over her and fresh tears pressed hard against the backs of her eyes. They were breaking up over a Christmas bazaar! Christmas. Christmas was less than two weeks away. She thought of the sapphire-blue hand-knit sweater she'd bought for Alec and tucked away in a gift box in her closet where the cats couldn't get at it. It would have gone so well with his eyes! She squeezed her own shut, tears still managing to spill over like water through a leaky dam.

Just when Kelsie was beginning to think Jules Verne had gone around the world in less time, they pulled up in front of the building where the bazaar was being held. She didn't jump out of the car. For a moment she sat staring at the crumpled tissue in her lap, trying to compose herself.

"I know this seems stupid to you," she said.

Alec held his tongue, too weary to give voice to any of the sharp retorts that came to mind.

"I love you, but I can't give up everything I've—" She had to pause to gulp for air. Tears fell to her lap, making dark spots on her faded denim jeans. "I can't depend on—oh, hell! Thanks for the ride," she said. Clutching her purse and her shredded tissues, she climbed out of the car and walked away.

ELEVEN

KELSIE SAT ON the floor of her living room wearing gray sweat pants and an old black sweater. She leaned back against the couch, a king-size box of tissues on one side of her, a five-pound box of assorted chocolates on the other. Her hair was a mess, and her eyes and nose were red and puffy from crying. It was Monday morning, the start of week two after her breakup with Alec. Jeff and Elizabeth were in school. As if they had sensed her need to be alone, her pets had disappeared. The drapes were closed. The radio muttered to itself in the background.

She'd never felt lower in her life. After her divorce she had been depressed, and, certainly, she had been terrified, but she had never felt like this, like fate had dropped an anvil on her head. She had lost Alec. She had lost the Van Bryant account. She was almost certainly going to lose her business.

The week after the infamous Humane Society bazaar incident had been dismal. She'd spent that week soul-searching and bursting into tears at the mere sight of a candy bar. However, it had been a productive week. She had come to some very important conclusions about herself and had resolved to get Alec back.

Alec had made a valid point about her reasons for joining all those groups she belonged to. It was true they had helped her establish her independence, but there was more to it. When her marriage had ended, she had needed involvement. Belonging to a group also had provided a measure of security. A volunteer organization couldn't find her lacking in any way, it would never cheat on her or leave her. No matter what happened in other areas of her life, it would always be there for her to cling to, the same way she clung to her sense of independence.

The trouble was, all the clubs and organizations in the world weren't going to fill the emptiness Alec's absence had left inside her. Independence was a great thing, but it couldn't put its arms around her or laugh with her or share her joy when she watched her son score a goal playing hockey.

She had been a coward. She'd been preparing herself for the end of her relationship with Alec before she'd even been involved with him.

What a fool she'd been. Alec wasn't Jack. Alec had charged to her rescue time and again. He had battered down her defenses and shown her how to have fun. She had almost forgotten what it was to feel like a woman—not just a mom or an agent or a chairperson, but a woman with passions and needs. Alec had shown her. He had given her his shoulder to lean on, his arms to protect her, his hand to guide her, his heart to love her. If any man deserved the title "knight in shining armor," it was Alec.

She'd been crazy to push him out of her life. They had found something special together, and she had been too big a coward to believe it could last.

Having made those discoveries about herself, Kelsie resolved to push aside her fears, to risk her pride and her heart and her damnable independence to prove to Alec how much she loved him, and to win him back.

If things had gone according to plan, she would have presented Alec with an apology and two very special gifts after the shooting of the first of the Darwin/Van Bryant ads. But things hadn't gone according to plan, and the letters of resignation she'd written to her groups and the blank calendar she'd hoped Alec would want to fill in with special times for the two of them to be together had been abandoned at the studio, left behind after Alec had thrown her and her client out.

She'd never seen him so angry. Of course, she reflected, he'd had every reason to be. As soon as the camera started to roll, Darwin had gone berserk on the set, attacked Eugene Van Bryant, destroyed several hundred dollars worth of props. The Van Bryant people had left shouting dire threats of lawsuits. Alec had been barely civil to Kelsie when she'd arrived, but she had seen the hurt beneath his controlled anger. After she and

Millard had finally gotten Darwin under control, the only thing she'd seen in Alec's eyes had been pure unadulterated fury.

"Everything that could go wrong went wrong," she said, biting into a mint. "They're going to have to start calling it Kelsie's Law; Murphy's got nothing on me."

She was going to lose the business she had worked so hard to build. Her commission on the Van Bryant account had been essential to the continuing operation of Monkey Business. Now, not only was she out the money, but she would probably be facing lawsuits from Van Bryant and Glendenning Advertising as well. The financial ramifications were not pleasant.

She sat staring at the Christmas tree she and the kids and Alec had put up the week after Thanksgiving. Even if it was only four days before Christmas, it looked terribly out of place, much too festive for the mood she was in. The brightly wrapped packages beneath it made her think only one thing: She had hit the limit on her credit cards. She'd had to dig through all the neatly arranged boxes to find the one from her great-aunt Lena—

the now unwrapped box of chocolates at her side. God bless Lena Lindberg, Kelsie thought, popping a bonbon into her mouth. She was nothing if not predictable.

No matter how hard she tried, it seemed her life was endlessly fouled up in one way or another. How did things go so wrong, she asked herself yet again. More important, what was she going to do about it? Step one was simple, she told herself as she pulled a section of the *Sunday Tribune* off the couch. She had to find a job. She paged through the classifieds, not really reading any of the ads.

She kept thinking that things wouldn't seem so bad if she hadn't lost Alec. If Alec were there to smile at her and put his arms around her, she could have found a lighter side to her bad luck. But Alec wasn't going to rescue her this time. She had never gotten the chance to apologize to him or tell him what he meant to her. Judging from the way he'd treated her on the set, it probably wouldn't have made any difference. He'd made it abundantly clear he was finished with her and her loony lifestyle.

She wondered for the hundredth time if he had

gotten in trouble over the Darwin disaster. Did vice-presidents lose their jobs over things like that, or only people like Steve Randall? Kelsie had tried all weekend to call Steve, but had spoken only to his answering machine.

"You've got to pull yourself together, Kelsie," she said aloud but with no conviction as she lifted another chocolate to her mouth.

She would pull herself together. She would dig herself out of this hole because she was a strong person, because she knew her children depended on her. First, however, she would allow herself the luxury of feeling miserable, of grieving for things lost and things that could never be, because she was human.

The fifth piece of chocolate—Kelsie had high hopes it was a caramel—was halfway to her mouth when the doorbell rang. At first she thought there was no one there. She looked from left to right. A jingling sound drew her gaze down. A brown spider monkey in a Santa suit stared up at her, offering her a small package wrapped in red and green plaid paper.

"Now, I know you didn't ring the bell, little

monkey," Kelsie said. "How'd you get here. Where's your accomplice?"

She looked up and down the street but didn't see a soul. The monkey chattered at her and jingled the bells on his suit, his long tail twitching in either nervousness or annoyance. When she took the package from him, he doffed his hat and gave her a toothy grin. Then a shrill whistle sounded and the monkey bounded off the steps, dashing to a brown sedan parked across the street. The car was gone before Kelsie could get a good look at the driver.

Closing the door, she looked down at the solid rectangular package. Who would be sending her a Christmas gift via a spider monkey? The tag gave no clue as to the identity of the gift giver, but instructed her to open it immediately. How strange, she thought, giving the thing a wary look. Slowly she lifted it to her ear and held her breath, listening.

"Oh, for Pete's sake," she grumbled. "You've really gone off the deep end if you think someone would actually have a monkey hand-deliver a bomb to you, Kelsie."

She dropped down on the couch and removed the wrapping from the package.

It was a videotape. There was no label explaining what was on the tape or why it had been given to her. There was no hint as to who had sent it. She popped it into her machine and turned the TV on, speculating all the while.

"Hello, I'm Eugene Van Bryant, president of Van Bryant Department Stores."

Kelsie's eyes nearly doubled in size. It was the beginning of the ill-fated ad they'd shot on Friday. Darwin raised his arms over his head, looked directly into the camera, and let loose a hair-curling shriek. Before he bounded out of Van Bryant's arms, he attacked the man's neatly combed white hair and set his glasses askew, then he went crazy. Kelsie watched the whole incredible scene unfold again, the camera focusing on the chimp's antics as he flung merchandise in every direction, swung from clothing racks, and dove headfirst into a bin of throw pillows.

Darwin exuberantly trashed what appeared to be a Van Bryant store to the tune of "Wipe Out." It was hysterically funny to her now that she was sitting in her living room watching it happen instead of on the set trying to catch the little monster. What was even funnier after having lived through the disaster was that it looked as if the whole thing had been planned. The occasional cutaway from the chimp to Mr. Van Bryant looking like the "nutty professor" was sheer genius. Kelsie was laughing so hard by the time the mini music video finished, she almost missed hearing the voice-over at the end—"Go ape at Van Bryant's."

That started another fit of laughter as she dragged herself off the couch to rewind the tape. She had to wipe the tears from her eyes with the back of her hand before she could see well enough to push the right button on the machine. An image of the disheveled Mr. Van Bryant came to mind, and she doubled over laughing, knocking her head on the edge of the television.

"Ouch! Oh! Go ape at Van Bryant's!" she said, gasping, her whole body jiggling like a gelatin mold run amok.

The doorbell rang before Kelsie had a chance to wonder what effect this piece of film might have on her life. Holding her stomach, she made her way across the living room. "Get a grip, Kelsie," she ordered herself, taking a deep breath before swinging the door open.

Alec stood on her front step wearing a Santa suit without the beard. Seeing him sobered Kelsie more quickly than a cold shower would have. A chill ran through her that had nothing to do with the frigid air pouring into the house from outside. Her heart began to hammer in her chest.

"Alec," she gasped.

"Merry Christmas," he said softly. His smile held the familiar, symmetrical tilt of his lips, hinting he knew all the most delicious secrets in the world—but there was something else there too. For the first time since she'd met him, Kelsie saw uncertainty in his smile, in the depths of his blue eyes. "Can I come in? I'm freezing my jingle bells off out here."

"Yes. Of course. Come in." She stepped back from the door, nerves forcing her to run a hand over her tangled hair. Her gaze swept the living room in a hasty reconnaissance. It looked like vandals had thrown a party, but there was nothing she could do about it now.

Alec closed the door behind him and looked

Kelsie straight in the eye. "Well? What do you think?"

What did she think about what, she wondered wildly. How he looked in a Santa suit? Wonderful, of course. She would have thought he looked wonderful in a clown suit.

"The Darwin video," he clarified, pulling off his Santa hat. Several strands of red-tinted dark hair fell across his forehead. "Did you like it?"

She'd been so stunned to see him, she completely forgot about the videotape. "Oh! Yes! You sent it? Where did you get the spider monkey?"

"Neillson's Petting Zoo. He's a client of yours." He didn't tell her he'd sent the monkey, because he thought she might have slammed the door in his face. He wouldn't have blamed her if she had, after the way he'd treated her.

"Nice touch," she said.

"Thanks." He could see she'd been crying and automatically blamed himself. Her hair needed combing; his fingers itched to touch it. Lord, how he'd missed her! Even when he'd been furious with her he had ached to hold her.

"The video was hysterical. Is it for real? I mean, are you really going to use it?"

"You bet. Steve Randall and I, and a very disgruntled film editor, worked all weekend on that baby. It took some doing to get Mr. Van Bryant to look at it, but once he did, he loved it. He laughed so hard, I thought we were going to have to give him oxygen. He's talking about putting the long version in movie theaters to run before the previews."

"That's wonderful." Kelsie smiled as she felt the financial noose loosen around her neck. "Millard will be relieved too."

"Millard will be rich," Alec corrected her. "Van Bryant is talking about doubling the amount of advertising he wants to do with this new campaign. He's even talking about using it as a springboard to launch new stores nationwide. Darwin is going to be a star, and that little beauty of a commercial is going to win Glendenning a Clio. See if it doesn't."

"You saved the day again," Kelsie said softly, thinking of how many times he had rushed to her rescue, her McKnight in shining armor.

A self-deprecating smile twisted his mouth. "I

saved my fanny from getting kicked onto the unemployment line too."

"I'm glad," Kelsie said with an uncertain smile.
She wanted to believe that hadn't been his only
reason for working around the clock on the new
idea but was afraid to put too much stock in her
hopes. She gave a little shrug. "I thought you'd
scrap the idea. I thought you hated it, and then
after what happened Friday—"

"I was wrong," he said simply, seriously. He
came forward and reached out a hand, running it
over her hair. His heart was in his throat. She had
every reason to toss him out, even if he had brought
good news. "I was wrong about a lot of things,
Kelsie. I acted like a world-class jerk on Friday. And
at the inn I said some pretty rotten things—"

"Some pretty true things too," she interrupted
quietly, looking down at his shiny black boots.

"I hurt you. Can you forgive me?"

She would have forgiven him anything; she
loved him so much. "You're forgiven," she murmured, wondering if this meant they could salvage
some part of the relationship they had torn to
shreds. There was only one way to find out. "I

wanted to tell you this on Friday, but...I was wrong, too, Alec. I didn't trust you enough to let go of my safety net of responsibilities. You were right, I am a coward. I hurt you. Can you forgive me?"

"I already have," he said, holding her gaze with his.

Kelsie was shaking inside and out. She was sure she saw love in his eyes. If she was wrong, she was going to fall hard, but it couldn't be any worse than what she'd gone through since they'd broken up. And if she was right... "Do you think we can start over?"

She thought she'd die when he shook his head, but then his arms were around her and he said, "I was hoping we could just pick up where we left off."

The kiss was like waking up safe and warm after a bad dream. Alec pulled her close, her nearness feeding his strength. Kelsie wrapped her arms around his neck. Her stomach fluttered as her knees buckled and her world suddenly tilted. Not even thinking of breaking contact with her mouth, Alec carried her to the couch and lowered her feet to the floor.

There were still things that needed to be said. They both knew it. But for the moment each of them needed the soothing reassurance of physical contact, physical love, to confirm what was in their hearts.

He pulled her sweater off over her head, barely breaking the rhythm of her fingers as she unbuttoned the red jacket of his costume, which joined her sweater on the floor. His skin was remarkably warm as her hands caressed his chest. His tongue found the shallow cup of her ear and dipped inside to tease her.

"Ever fantasize about making it with Santa?" he asked in his satiny voice.

"Too kinky, Alec," she said, nipping at his collarbone.

He chuckled wickedly. "You think so? How about with one of Santa's helpers?"

Kelsie giggled, then gasped as his hands found her breasts. He cupped them together, bent and pressed a kiss to each before letting his fingers roam to the drawstring of her sweat pants.

"I love these things," he said, plucking at the bow. "They're so easy to get into." A groan rose up from deep in his throat when he slid his hands inside the soft fabric to cup her bottom. "And do you know what it does to me when I find out you aren't wearing any panties? It drives me wild."

"They're like pajamas to me," she explained breathlessly. "I don't see any need to—"

"I wasn't complaining."

"Oh. Ohhhh . . . Alec, you're so naughty."

"Yeah, but I doctored Santa's list, so I'm still getting presents."

The sweat pants dropped to the floor, joining the sweater and jacket. Kelsie raised up on tiptoe, her mouth seeking and finding his. She kissed him as deeply as she knew how, her tongue sliding in to caress his mouth as his hand slid over the silky curve of her hip.

A wolf whistle sounded from the far corner of the dining room. "Love me, baby. Love me, baby. Love me, baby."

Their groans were a duet of mutual frustration.

"Have you given any serious consideration to baking that bird for Christmas dinner?" Alec asked as Kelsie grabbed up his red Santa jacket and slipped it on.

"What kind of stuffing do you prefer?"

"Oyster," he said, admiring the way the jacket barely covered her bottom as she went to the parrot's cage and dropped the cloth cover over it. When she came back to him, he wrapped his arms around her lightly and said, "Anyone can see we belong together."

"You think so?" she asked, feeling pleasantly lightheaded. She traced the arc of his smile with her fingertip.

"Oh, yes. We're *well suited*," he said, tugging at the white fur trim of the jacket.

She barely had time to groan and roll her eyes before he pulled her down on top of him on the couch.

"I believe we have some unfinished business with this piece of furniture," he said, vividly recalling the night he had taken Jeffrey to the hockey game and how he and Kelsie had played on the couch afterward until they were interrupted.

"Mmm, yes, I—ouch! What have you got in this jacket pocket?" she asked, arching up to save herself from getting jabbed again.

"Pocket? Oh! I almost forgot." He dug into the

pocket and produced two small gift-wrapped packages. "Two more early Christmas presents for you. Open this one first."

They sat up side by side, and Alec watched and held his breath as Kelsie unwrapped a diamond and sapphire engagement ring.

"I figured this would solve a few of our scheduling problems," he said softly as she stared at the ring in open-mouthed shock.

"Alec," she said. "I don't know what to say."

"There you go again, letting me know your weaknesses. Say yes. That's what I want to hear."

"Are you sure?" she asked, looking deep into his eyes for her answer. "You know it's not just me you'll be marrying, Alec. Jeffrey and Elizabeth—"

"I think Jeffrey and Elizabeth are terrific kids."

"And the dog and the rabbits and the fish and the parrot and the cats?"

"I really like Jeffrey and Elizabeth." He broke into a grin at her look of disappointment because he hadn't included her pets in his statement. "Honey, I don't care if I have to adopt the whole damn Minnesota Zoo. I love you. And if this last week has been a preview of what my life would be like without you, I know I couldn't stand it."

Tears spilled over the rim of Kelsie's lashes and caught on the corners of her smile. "I love you too."

Tenderly Alec brushed the crystal drops away. "Think you can stand being married to a neat freak who wants to spend all his spare time with his arms around you?"

She tried to laugh and nodded her head, wiping away more tears. Alec leaned over and pressed a kiss to her trembling lips.

"Open your other present," he ordered.

Kelsie slipped her ring on first. It was a tad large, but that hardly spoiled the moment. Then she carefully untaped the wrapping on the small flat box. Inside, on a bed of white satin was an expensive-looking gold pen.

"A pen. You romantic devil. This sure tops the engagement ring," she said dryly. "It's lovely, Alec, but I'm not sure I understand the significance."

He traced a finger over the eyebrows he found so sexy. "Friday you left a calendar at the studio for me. Whether you meant to leave it or not, after what happened, I don't know. Inside the cover you wrote that it would remain blank until I filled it in."

He lifted the pen and tapped it against the end of her upturned nose. "I thought it would be a better idea if we filled it in together. That way we can both make time for what's important. Sometimes it'll be work. Sometimes it'll be the kids." He smiled. "Sometimes it might even be the Humane Society. All are important, but in our hearts we'll know we will always take time for each other—starting with a honeymoon," he added with a devilish grin.

Kelsie laughed and agreed.

In unison they said, "*That's* what's *really* important!"

They shared a kiss, a kiss full of promise.

"Merry Christmas, sweetheart," he whispered, holding her close.

As Alec drew her back down on the couch with him, Kelsie murmured against his lips, "You make a good knight in shining armor, Mr. Mc-Knight, but you're also a great Santa."

Alec gave her a wily smile and pinched her bottom. "Ho ho ho."